Reaching Sky

Alinar Den

Published by Alinar Den, 2024.

This is a work of fiction. Similarities to real people, places, or events are entirely coincidental.

REACHING SKY

First edition. February 29, 2024.

Copyright © 2024 Alinar Den.

ISBN: 979-8224870431

Written by Alinar Den.

It may not be my story to tell, but I want to do it while I still remember. Life is so unpredictable... You never know when you forget something important, like it never existed. Sometimes it just slips away, but I'm ready to fight for it, for every moment, for every word.

She is my dangerous secret, my mystery, my evidence of craziness... Knowing her, being next to her, created a new world inside of me.

"If you don't want to eat burnt pancakes, please open the door." I was never good at cooking, so it sounded like a real threat. "And please be nice... at least this time..."

Sky had her ups and downs with unplanned visitors. One day extremely polite to even undeserving individuals, another day she was jumping on them like a wild animal, ready to shred random strangers into ribbons.

Sky nodded and slid down from the high bar chair. She loved sitting on this extremely uncomfortable chair watching me swearing and burning our food. I believe this picture of me, struggling with cooking, was giving her a feeling of home, family, safety maybe... if an occasional fire alarm can be called safe...

She was reading when someone knocked at the door or was pretending to read. Hiding behind the book was something she did a lot even while being a little girl, shielding herself from the world, not bothering to see what it offers.

I usually make an effort not to stare at her while she is reading, but every time I see her absorbed by a book, it reminds me of the day we met.

It happened in an orphanage, during one of those charity events, when your company decides to spend their money on something good. I never volunteered before because the idea of being surrounded by kids... scared me to death...

I have an excuse though... My first experience with it was slightly traumatic. I was in my early 20's, working at my first ever job. My company decided to organize a charity event in an orphanage and to bring along girls who already made their living by entertaining kids (it was our actual job - hosting kids' birthday parties). We just needed to do everything we did daily: keep kids entertained... Sounded easy enough. The audience was supposed to be 5 or even 10 times bigger than usual, which could be a challenge, but we were up to it. Young and ambitious.

Yes, audience size was not the main issue at all. What our bosses failed to tell us before we arrived there, was that kids were not only orphans (which was not an issue!), kids were sick...

I barely remember the room we entered, only that it was huge and reminded me of school theater. Probably it was not such a significant interior compared to a big picture.

You probably guessed it by now. The kids were sick. Some of them mentally, some physically, most of them clinging to wheelchairs. They were really happy to see us, probably not having much entertainment, the atmosphere was hospital or even prison like there.

I still remember the moment my coworker and I looked at each other, realization hit us. We had bags stuffed with items for active kids' games. The only items we were able to use now out of our inventory were small paper flags, to waive and attract attention. I will never forget how I was trying to give one of the flags to a child in a wheelchair and he spread his leg to pick it up with his toes, unable to do it with his crooked fingers.

We did the best we could to keep the energy high, our smiles up and our audience entertained. On our way back me and my partner were sitting in the car, not able to talk to our boss, who set us up so badly. Each of us stared through the passenger side windows, silently trying to hide the tears streaming down our cheeks. Deep inside I was struggling with a heartbreaking picture of poor kids mixed with raving rage. They didn't warn us, they didn't bother to, or they were just afraid we would reject the offer knowing the truth.

As much as I wanted to forget this experience, it was still there after years, reaching out to me every time kids related charity events were planned… like that child in a wheelchair.

So, that was my first orphanage visit experience. Still wondering why the idea of doing it again was not flying with me? The first one broke me badly…

I would be happy to purely blame it on my PTSD, but even before that colorful experience I never wanted to become a mother. Phrases like "Oh, you're still young" or "You didn't meet the right guy yet" only made me smile. If I tried to explain that I simply am not a fan of kids and never wanted one, people just couldn't accept it. How is it possible that a young, smart and successful woman doesn't want to get married and have a child? So, usually when the conversations about kids started, I simply nodded when someone was telling me that it's not my time yet. Nodding helps to change the subject, also if you pretend sad or even crying, they mostly shut the f*ck up. I was good at it before, having scenarios for different people, like an actress. Sometimes playing along is easier. What's the point of arguing with a "happy mother of two little angels" regarding life choices?

I heard it somewhere before: "Getting a child is like putting a tattoo on your face. It's highly visible and it is for all your life." Try to say it to a "happy mother", you probably would get an intense reaction.

So, years later, after deep and paranoid research of the orphanage we were going to, I finally said "yes" to this terrifying offer. Look at me trying to beat emotional trauma! Maybe I just needed to stick a new picture on top of the old faded one on my wall of memories. Maybe that's where I was meant to be. Probably both.

I was not even supposed to be there, I was just covering for my colleague as she became sick right before this visit. My boss made an effort to convince me that it's good for my career to take part in this kind of event and I thought "What can go wrong?"... Like I had something better to do on Saturday... Young, smart, successful and very single at the time. One thing was true, I didn't date the right guy then.

They had a plan. Toys, games, food, gifts, kids' performances... all the regular stuff, I guess. It was going smoothly, but I was looking for a dark corner to hide from all of it from the moment I stepped into the building. It was not horrible; I just couldn't do it. After one hour of fake smiling and pretending to be having a fun time, I faked a phone call and hid in one of the bedrooms to answer it. Was it fate to choose the right door in an unfamiliar building? It could be a broom closet for what I know, but it wasn't... It was her bedroom.

I remember how I flinched, not expecting someone else to be in the room, thinking that every single soul, except me, was having fun at the party.

Later I found out that she was 4 years old, but my initial thought was that she was 6 or 7 at least. She was tiny, she didn't look older, but the picture didn't really match. Sky was sitting on her bed, reading a book that was bigger than the girl herself. Not one of these colorful children's books. This one even looked huge and boring, like history or philosophy... no pictures at all! It was not something you normally see in the hands of a tiny girl. I never saw an adult reading such a book, not talking about a 4-year-old! That's why my brain was shocked and tried to convince me that she was older.

She looked into my eyes, and I felt goosebumps all over my body. For a few seconds she was curious, checking out my hand holding the phone and smiling. Like she knew something I didn't, like she had a plan. And that was it. After that she lost her interest and continued reading.

All those kids around were so lonely, clingy, craving for attention, genuine and friendly... and here was Sky. Probably because she was so different, I decided to approach her. I was intrigued.

I stepped closer to her, no reaction followed. Her tiny finger kept sliding through the dusty page. I took one more step for her to look up again. And it happened again: my goosebumps, her curiosity for a few seconds and... she lost interest again... That huge book apparently was way more exciting than I was.

I heard the door opening behind my back. The nurse was standing in the doorway. "Not going to work if you're expecting a dialog, Dear" she said sarcastically. "Sky is... different."

She sounded like she had a secret on her mind but was not sure if she could trust me with it.

"What do you mean?" That was the only question I had, the only thing I wanted to know.

"You better go back." The nurse made up her mind about trusting me. Was she protecting the little girl's privacy, or was it planned to spike my interest? I guess we'll never know. I had no choice but to come back to "enjoying myself" at the party.

Everything I could think of for the next couple of days was that tiny girl with the most beautiful eyes I've ever seen. I will never be able to erase that day from my memory, the day when Sky put a brick into the foundation of my life.

The memory flow stopped as soon as I heard his voice:

"I told you already. If your mother decides to cook, let me know and I'll bring something edible." Dave was standing in front of me, gracefully balancing two paper cups in one hand.

"Thank you for believing in my culinary skills, Hon!"

"I will take my words back if you tell me that none of the pancakes got burned." He knew me better than I thought, but he would never check for the bodies of fallen pancake soldiers, hidden in the garbage the moment he rang the doorbell.

Sky couldn't hold a laugh, trying to hide her face behind the book. It was barely audible, but I saw her eyes lighten up, the expression I've seen so many times before and would love to see as many times as possible in the future.

Dave was my first boyfriend she actually liked, the first guy who stepped into our lives with ease. My previous boyfriends were trying to connect with Sky, sometimes making an effort of buying their way into her heart (which didn't work) ... Dave didn't. Sky was never his main girl to charm. He didn't try to please a child to win points from her mother. He just cared about me and was there when I needed him. I didn't even realize when and how it got him a seat behind the family table. Both me and Sky just took Dave in, and he became something more than just a friend in the blink of an eye.

"It is my day off and I will start it by burning a few pancakes and having the best coffee in town!" I took a paper coffee cup from Dave's hand acting like my life depended on it.

"Brought here by the best boyfriend?" Dave tried to kiss me. I felt blush popping up on my cheeks. It was still weird to kiss him in front of Sky. She looked at me with a familiar expression, like she knew something I didn't.

• • • •

As you probably understood already, Sky became a part of my life since that weird orphanage day. One week after the event I went back there. Just couldn't stop thinking about the little girl and the nurse that wouldn't tell me her secret.

The nurse seemed friendlier this time, shaking my hand and smiling. She sat next to me on the couch in the reception area.

"Pam... You can call me Pam" she said. She was breathing heavily. It seemed like it took her a huge effort to get there. She was a bit overweight, and it was obviously making her life difficult. It was probably not easy to deal with all those kids when she had a hard time moving faster than walking.

"My name is Ace" I was looking at Pam, wondering why her attitude had changed. "I just wanted to ask you..."

She had her question ready before I finished mine: "Are you writing a story?"

"No... I was a part of a group at a charity event."

"I remember you, Dear. Ask your questions. I don't have much time." And why did her smile disappear now?

"I was thinking about the girl I saw that day... Sky..." My mouth was completely dry, my skin burning. For a second, I started to dream about a cold shower... Or a swimming pool. I didn't know how to ask the question, which had been bothering me for a week. "Can you tell me about her?" God, that sounded so stupid. I felt so miserable.

"Ace... It's the first time I hear this name."

I nodded. Not the first time I heard these words. I didn't tell her how often people said it before. She didn't have much time, right?

She continued saying "She liked you".

My eyes open wider. The girl that barely paid attention to me liked me. Why?

Pam read my confusion and continued talking without question being asked. "As I told you before, Sky is different. She doesn't communicate as other kids do. She doesn't speak".

Wow. That was disappointing. Was it THE secret? This girl is different only because she is not talking. And I spent one week thinking about her, wondering... But she is so young. Do the kids normally speak at this age? Is it so rare?

Pam saw all this in my face again and continued her speech. "You look disappointed, Dear. Don't be. The small one is so special and smart, probably better than any adult I know." She sounded mysterious.

"How do you know?" I didn't even think before I asked a question.

Pam handed me a note, safely kept in her apron until now.

"She wrote a note for you." Pam concluded.

I saw a clear printed handwriting and read the sentence with my vision blurring "Acelia. She will come back for me."

I felt goosebumps attack again. No one called me by that name for years. For as long as I remember I was going for "Ace" and loved it.

"Can I see her?" I was not feeling that nervous before my job interviews... or first dates...

"Did you make an appointment?" Pam looked serious now. God, this woman was so complicated to read. For a moment I thought that she was going to kick me out of the orphanage. But the look on her face changed and she started laughing. It looked like she didn't have enough air as she started coughing and choking, while still laughing. For the short second I wanted to help her, offer water, but when I realized that she was teasing me... oh, yeah... she deserved it.

"Sorry dear, you just looked so serious, like you wanted to meet a president, not a 4-year-old." Pam continued laughing, but without coughing this time. My eyebrows moved up. I bit my lip. This lady was evil, but she was right, I guess.

"Ok, ok" Pam finally calmed down, her face red and sweaty from exhausting laughter. "Follow me."

She stood up and walked slowly and silently through familiar doors and corridors. At that moment I realized that my life is going to change forever.

· · · ·

About a week after Dave gloriously saved my day off with coffee, I was watching something on TV, browsing through my social media and eating chips at the same time. Modern multitasking as a survival skill!

Sky rushed downstairs from her room, she looked happy and glorious, like she finally killed a boss or a dragon or whatever she was slaying in her videogames. But not this time. She was happy about something else. I knew it, because for a moment her glorious look faded as she studied me carefully, reading me. I recognized it because for 10 years she did it every single time she wanted to ask me about something and was not sure how I would react.

But it was only for a moment. I smiled. As always, she looked like she knew more than I did. It felt this way next to her annoyingly often.

"Show me." I was looking at the paper in her hand. She didn't write it by herself, Sky stopped communicating with pen and paper since mobile phones were invented. It was something important, but I knew that I sorted out all the formalities at school already... I started reading, curiously.

"Permission... Blah blah... Rope jumping for underage... Ha-ha! Since when do you need my permission? You didn't ask me that when you went to that drunk party in Ben's house... And ended up punching a huge guy in the face! I will not save you from the police this time, little lady!"

I was serious for a split second and started laughing at once, watching guilt developing on her face.

"That's what a normal parent would say? Right?" I acted like I was getting a reward for the best parenting, seeing her fake cheering and applauding.

I never was a normal parent, never could, never had a chance... You cannot be a normal parent to an abnormal child... Abnormal, is it even a word? Should I rather say 'different'?

Sky pulled her phone out of her pocket and started texting. Sue's voice told me "He was not that huge..."

Sue sounded mostly like a GPS guide, pronouncing words clearly but without any bit of understanding of their meaning in the sentence. Sue was the voice from the app that talked everything Sky was typing, and we actually liked her better than Greg. I remember those few days of laughter when Sky sounded like a guy in a leather jacket next to a fancy night club. Of all the voices in the app Sue was the best option, trust me.

"Not huge compared to what!? To a bear?"

Sky smiled. She looked proud of herself. I'm still wondering how she even managed to punch him, according to Ben's description he looked twice as big as her... Yeah, Sky was tinier than most kids of her age. She was small and skinny, wearing ripped jean shorts and an oversize t-shirt which was way oversized if you ask me... I think it belonged to my ex, by the way. Hmmm... Never mind. It doesn't look like he's getting it back, not from her.

She put her hand up to her hair and pulled a pen out of it. Silver locks dropped on her shoulders as the pen was the only thing holding them up. Her hair was so messy, probably not even brushed, straight and wavy at the same time, fizzy from the humid weather. It looked like it had its own character, wild and stubborn, same as the owner. Surprisingly, it looked extremely healthy and shiny, even though Sky was ignorant about any possible hair routines.

I still remember that morning, when my 11-year-old Sky stepped into my room looking confused. Day before she fell asleep with brown locks on her pillow and the next morning she was standing in front of my bed with completely gray hair. When she woke me up, I thought I was dreaming at first, seeing a silver headed angel, but later I recognized my girl. It took time to get used to it. Sky refused to dye hair back brown, she said she liked it better this way. It was special now, matching her perfectly. It took her a few hours to realize how she should look like now, what clothing style would match... It took me years to realize that my daughter knows what she wants from her life better than I do.

"You will not jump" Vic looked serious saying this.

Sky was standing next in the queue. All the skydiving equipment was already on her body. She was staring at her shoes, waiting for the moment when Vic would escort her to the edge and she finally jumps from this bridge, making her dream come true. Girl won the war for doing it, getting all the necessary papers for this single moment to come. She had my blessing. To tell you the truth, it wasn't hard to get. I never could stop her from doing anything she wanted, especially something well planned for months, something she dreamed of. What to do, I was the mother who did more crazy and stupid stuff than her daughter. The small one was definitely wiser than I was at her age.

Thinking she didn't hear him, Vic decided to repeat "Hey, small one. Wait a second, step aside, give way to the person behind you. You will not jump."

He heard Tom's voice behind him: "It's ok bro, she is underage, but she has a permission."

"I'm not talking about permission, she is not ready. Too scared." Vic wanted to wave to the guy standing behind Sky to come closer, but something stopped him.

He was working with Tom's team as a rope jumping instructor for more than a year already and he recognized different types of jumpers... Jump addicted, first timers, screaming, silent, couples in love, scared... quitters, the ones that wouldn't jump, taking their money back and leaving, giving up on the dream. Vic secretly despised quitters, he didn't know how you could do it, be on a final step, reach the edge of the bridge and suddenly become too scared to do it. It was a weakness, Vic didn't understand or accept it, being a born leader. Since he was a child all kids respected him, even older ones didn't mess with him. There was always something in him, something dangerously attractive, almost hypnotizing, making people follow his lead blindly.

From the moment he saw Sky, he just knew that she was one of those quitters. Too small to even be visible behind the person standing in front of her in a queue, too young... She was staring at her shoes, like it was more interesting than the amazing view from the bridge, more exciting than talking to people around. She was like a gray spot in a colorful crowd, moving slowly like a prisoner in the line, waiting for her turn. She didn't look up until he started talking to her. That was how he knew that this teenager would not be able to jump. She looked and seemed too weak to do it.

Normally he didn't tell people straight, giving them a chance to quit themselves, but today he was not in the mood. Partly his mind was not there. It was with Val, who stood behind him, obviously flirting with Tom. She was doing it to annoy Vic, to make him jealous. He knew that and it didn't make him jealous, it made him angry. He made a mistake once by sleeping with Val and now she was all around his friends, expecting that he would become jealous enough to do it again. Val didn't want Tom or anyone else, she needed Vic, probably too desperately... Why did he even care? She was the live evidence of his weakness, and he hated it. Even being drunk that night was not an excuse.

For a second, Vic turned around, looking back at Toms' happy face and then back to Sky, ready to call in the next jumper, skipping the child. He froze, feeling freezing goosebumps appearing on his skin on this extremely hot summer day. She was standing right in front of him, looking straight in his eyes. For a few seconds Vic just couldn't find words, hating himself even more now for being this way.

But... the 'Child' was the most beautiful woman he ever saw in his life. Her big eyes were silverish gray, matching her platinum hair locks, popping from under the hood. The way she looked at him made his heart stop, his body didn't belong to himself, nor his voice. Stunned... He never felt this way before.

Sky looked at Val. It seemed like she understood what Vic was angry about, smiling with the corner of her mouth. One more look into his eyes, checking if she didn't miss anything, and that was it. Now she was holding everything about Vic in her small fist. All his strength and alfa nature felt blurry, like it never existed. The girl was angry... One moment ago, Vic felt like a giant next to a tiny girl, now he felt like a bug under her shoe, and she was the one making a decision to squeeze life out of him or to keep him alive.

It could not be right. It did not make sense at all. She kept looking straight in his eyes and he felt hypnotized by the silver glow she was projecting. It was just his imagination and deep inside he knew it.

Guy behind Sky became inpatient "No worries, man, take your time, stare as much as you want. We're just all waiting for our turn here".

Vic realized that he had been silent for too long, doing or at least saying something was crucial now. He squeezed his fist just to find out if he is paralyzed the way he felt. No, he was not, muscles moved with unexpected ease. Sky reached for her phone, zipped inside her pocket.

He really needed to say something, and it sounded broken: "How old are you?"

Sue answered almost at once as Sky probably predicted this question: "Fourteen. He has my permission". She pointed at Tom.

"Oh." Vic was even more confused now. He started to talk a bit louder and slower. "Are you sure you are ready to jump?"

Sky looked even angrier now, but Sue was still talking in a regular mechanical way. "I am not deaf, you idiot." Once again, he felt overpowered, like a bug under her shoe, maybe even tinier now.

"I'm... sorry." Vic didn't even realize why he said it. He was not sorry, terribly intrigued, desperate for a solution, but not sorry. He nodded and shook his head trying to remove this untypical feeling of weakness.

The dialog was not going to happen. Sky hid the phone back in the pocket, demonstrating that she didn't want to talk to Vic anymore and spread her hands, letting him make the final equipment preparations, by attaching rope to her vest. Surprisingly for Vic, she stepped onto the platform on the edge of the bridge without a shade of hesitation. Now she finally was admiring the view around her, taking it all in. Sky turned back, looking at Vic with a vivid smile. She won and he was defeated, and they both felt it.

The girl spread her hands and jumped, like she had been doing it all her life. Natural, confident, gracious, with zero hesitation. Vic heard people in the crowd applauding. It was beautiful. She was perfect...

Guy that was standing behind Sky couldn't help but notice "And you said she will not jump. The child just kicked your ass, bro".

This was the moment Vic met Sky.

I wouldn't say that he was her kryptonite, her hardest challenge... Or maybe I should... Yeah, probably it is correct... Kryptonite is a good word for it.

• • • •

I had a lovely day at work. One of those days when everything goes smoothly, you don't have any extreme problems and your phone does not ring every single second. I even had my break today, managing to eat without interruption... It sounds disturbing, but I rarely have days like this at work.

I am a workaholic, and I was working too hard then. I was just still getting used to my promotion and my colleagues were still absorbing the fact that I'm a big boss now and they need to take their own responsibilities sometimes, make their own decisions. Some people don't like to take on responsibilities. I know that it is easier to push weight on someone else's shoulder, than to carry it. Even before promotion I had multiple calls per day with colleagues asking for advice. Most of the time, they wanted me to make decisions for them. I didn't mind it; I was always ready to help.

What bothers me still is how people are afraid to fail, to be wrong. I messed up many times in my life, pulling through complications I created with my own hands, admitting to myself and others that I messed it up. I had tons of cases when I needed to stop panicking, put myself together and create an action plan. I learned from it, and it pulled my introvertive ass out of the shell. I'm still a big mess, but I know how to fix it. I know my strengths and weaknesses. That's why I was the one getting promotion despite the fact that I was the youngest and the least experienced manager in the team. That's what Dave's ex-boss, who is my current boss now, told me while offering a promotion, and I believed him.

So, this was one of those days when I believed that life could be easy, and work doesn't need to be stressful. But I also felt that everything cannot just go so smoothly, and something bad is going to happen. Don't judge me, I swear I'm a positive thinker most of the time!

The first thing I saw when I came home was an opened book. Sky was reading something, and she left it on the bar counter. Book looked like it was at least a hundred years old, with yellowish pages and worn-out cover, like it came straight from the restricted book section of Hogwarts library. Only God knows where Sky was getting those antiques from... The book was open, and it was the moment when I realized that my day would not be good anymore. My daughter never left books open like this. Once she told me that if she leaves the book open, the story can run away. For the record, this book looked like it could release something nasty... When she said it, she was 7, but she sounded so confident that I believed her. She was always a book expert in the family.

Sometimes I felt jealous when Sky was reading, she looked at the pages with such attention and with such passion. She watched the books. Stories and texts came to life, and she sensed them, totally absorbed by action. I saw it in her eyes when I first met her. That tiny child was not reading a book, she was living through it.

And this book was opened...

I stepped closer to the bar counter and glanced at it, hoping that no scary stories would run away. My imagination was already drawing, how Sky was accidentally sucked inside this one and now she is trapped. Hmm. This weekend's 'Harry Potter movie marathon' really did affect me.

I looked around. Sky was sitting on the couch covered with a blanket, watching TV. I had never seen her doing it before... Alone at least. She did it to spend time with me, or Dave, or Ben. But TV was never on my daughter's list of interests. Why do you need TV when you have that creepy ancient book, which was unfortunately still open a few steps behind me? I tried to calm down my wild imagination and started the actual conversation with her:

"Sky... Baby, you left that book open... Oh..."

In response, I saw eyes full of tears. This was not a spontaneous desire to watch the news, she was hiding from something, desperately trying to distract her mind. If she couldn't even focus on the book, it was bad.

"I need to know, Sky... Please, I really need to know if you threw someone from that bridge..."

She smiled with the corner of her lips. I appreciated it. At least she was ready to talk about it, at least that's what I thought.

"Please don't tell me it's that huge guy again. Is he alive?"

Sky shook her head, like she was only now realizing that I'm truly crazy. She blinked and a small tear ran down her cheek.

"What can I do?" I was serious now.

She shook her head again. There was nothing I could do to help her.

• • • •

Drinking was not a bad idea. Vic was staring at the empty whiskey glass in front of him on the table, ice slowly melting inside of it.

Bar was full of people who were drinking, laughing, fighting... drinking again. It created a sort of background noise.

"Are you ok, bro?" Tom looked concerned. He was always worried about the team, being like a father to naughty kids. Tom was the kind of person who asked questions and really wanted to know answers. He had a good soul, ready to help and support, knowing how it felt when no one was there for you. Tom was lonely, but he found himself by being there for others, for his team especially. And it was his best chance to talk to them. Day out. A few days off were ahead of all the team, so it was time to rest, enjoy and get drunk. Last time after this day Vic woke up with Val in his bed.

"I am, I guess." Vic lied the best he could.

"What happened with that teen girl today?" It seemed like Tom was reading his mind.

Vic shook his head. What could he say? That the tiny girl made him feel like no other woman did before? That she just squeezed his heart in her tiny hand and jumped with it to the river? Literally... What the hell was it? How did... He was ashamed of himself, looking this way at a minor, feeling this way next to her, being weak. It was so out of character, so confusing. But drinking helped to slow down these piercing thoughts.

Val came back, putting glasses with fresh drinks on the table. Place was crowded, so she used her magic and got drinks by herself from the bar, not waiting for the server to be free. Male bartenders would never say 'no' to her. She was using her magic on all of them when the team went out. It worked, what to say. You needed to be blind or gay not to want Val. This long dark hair, tanned skin, tattoos all over her beautiful body... She was the kind of girl you can find on the Playboy pages. Guys looked hungry when she was around. Extreme, addicted jumper. That's how she became a part of their team... This and the money. Val was dealing with money and doing it well, unique ability for a pretty woman. She was the only girl in a team and truly enjoyed it, absorbing attention like her life depended on it.

Vic looked around, studying people in the bar. He could read them, at least he thought he could do it. Fancy looking ladies sitting on the bar chairs, waiting for someone to join them. A group of nerds on the corner couch probably discussing how drunk the ladies need to be to sleep with them. A couple on a first date feeling awkward and worried. A bunch of guys with lots of beers... They were the ones who kept female servers occupied. What to say, those guys were damn good looking, probably military.

"Yummy" Val was looking in the same direction as Vic. She was biting her juicy bottom lip. "Especially that one, in a black t-shirt."

"Get him!" Vic couldn't stop himself from saying it like a dog command.

"That is one horny Val…" Tom was staring at water drops sliding to the bottom of his still full bear glass. Yep, one soldier down. Tom was drunk already.

"Honey, if I wanted a cutie in black, I would have him." Val sounded confident enough and Vic couldn't help but challenge her.

"So, what stops you?" Vic knew she was drunk enough to accept the challenge. He knew her that well.

Val stood up, took her drink and a few seconds later noisy guys became much more interested in her, than in waitresses. But Val was not that lucky. A few moments after she took a seat next to the "cutie", his phone rang and he rushed away, trying to hear the person who was calling him through the bar noise. Val was disappointed, Vic only smiled.

His attention was attached to a guy in a black t-shirt as Vic involuntarily heard pieces of his phone conversation. "I'm out with guys" … "Do you want me to come over?" … "Let me know if you need anything at all…" "I love you too…"

Vic smiled even wider now, apparently Val's chances were not that high with this one. Vic looked at his whiskey glass. "Hmm, double this time. It felt like someone wants to make me drunk again."

• • • •

"Still in her room?" Dave came to me holding a familiar coffee cup in his hands. "I didn't expect to find you here…"

Tell me about it… I was sitting on a sun lounge, next to the swimming pool.

"Yep, here I am, tanning next to the pool when my daughter is in her room trying to sort out the issue she is not even telling me about. Am I a horrible parent?"

Dave smiled, letting me take coffee from his hand.

"I'm not sure that someone was ever a better mother to a child..."

"...that is not even hers?" I interrupted impatiently. I sounded upset. I was.

"Not what I wanted to say, Babe".

"I know, sorry... It's the second day already and I keep wondering if I'm doing the right thing..."

"You tried to go there, did you?"

"And found her detached from this world, meditating. And now I'm here, hoping that she will see me in the window and come downstairs."

"You're not the only one who is hoping." Dave pointed at the third cup in the holder.

"Did I ever thank you?" I was trying my best not to take Dave for granted. All this support and caring felt so natural coming from him. It made him special, unique even. I never met a guy who was worried about me so much.

I took a sip of coffee and rolled my eyes. "Even THIS is not right."

Dave took a sip as well and his face changed. Even coffee didn't taste good. I took my phone from the small table and started typing to the manager on duty. "Please check your coffee."

I wanted to add something angry but realized that it will not do much good. I couldn't lose my shit now, not on them...

"Did you ever have a feeling that if you're not at work, everything is f*cked up there?"

He smiled. He didn't need to answer. Dave was promoted from my position only a few months ago, the same day when I was offered to do the job. He knew...

That was also the day when our relationship officially started. Did I get this job by sleeping with Dave? No. Did I want to sleep with him when he was my direct boss? Hell, yeah! Apparently, he also wanted it, probably that's why he agreed to leave the place which was his for so many years. That's what I wanted to believe in at least. I never asked though.

Now it doesn't matter. He is working in a different hotel, but still comes to mine to get the best coffee in town, mostly for me and my daughter.

"I just want her to be OK. I hope she will..."

I was not able to finish the sentence, hearing something behind me. Dave and I turned at the same time. Sky was standing in the doorway, looking a bit pale, with a sprinkle of red around her nose, like when you have the flu... Or nosebleed. OMG, now I knew what she was doing in her room. Now I knew how serious it was.

"Is it Ok now?"

Sky shrugged. Dave didn't understand a thing, looking confused. I knew only that for these days my daughter was trying to remove memories from someone's mind. I hope it was necessary. If it was, I hope it worked...

* * * *

"Oh, shit. What the hell was in that drink?" Vic was talking to his own reflection looking in a mirror.

He did it again. Woke up in bed and found Val sleeping next to him. "You need to stop drinking, man." He said pointing a finger to the mirror.

He barely remembered what happened between them... at least that didn't change. But he did remember the weird feeling of forgetting something important. It felt like when you went to the shop to buy something because you urgently needed it, but ended up browsing shelves with no idea why you were there. Vic splashed freezing water from the tab on his face. Headache was a killer. He pointed finger to his reflection again and added "And I'm serious about drinking!"

"Vic... Who are you talking to?"

Now she was awake. Good job.

He stepped into the room feeling awkward. She was lying in bed, partly covered with the blanket... Only partly. Vic was silently swearing at his animal nature. He was trying to find in his memories the part when Val left those guys and came back to him. Nothing came up, everything looked blurry. From all the guys in that bar she ended up in his bed. Again. Any other would be proud of himself. Was he? Not now, not when it happened the first time. He didn't want Val with his heart, never did, never would.

Vic spent a few more seconds thinking of what he should do with the woman in his bed. Last time he told her it would not happen again. What should he tell her now?

"Hungry?"

"Omg, Vic, will you even cook for me?"

"Yes, Babe, you finally have what you wanted. You've got me. But there is this thing, I will not pretend to be your boyfriend and play games. You have two options: we will have breakfast, aspirin, small conversation about our painful hangover... and you will leave. Or you will get up right now and get your ass out of my apartment. What will you choose?" Vic demonstrated two decisions by imaginary weighing them on his empty palms.

"Screw you, Victor!"

"Valerie... We are not friends, not lovers, and let's try to keep it not enemies either."

Vic was trying to calm her down, but apparently Val was expecting a kiss on the neck and words of love. She was angrily pacing across the room, looking for her clothes.

Standing with his hands folded, Vic asked with an evil smile "No breakfast then?"

He was teasing her, and it worked, Val looked at him with furious eyes.

"I have only one question to ask you..."

Vic was expecting something like "Why are you such a jerk?" or "Did your mother teach you to treat women like this?", but it never came.

"Who is she and why you cannot f*ck her? Why did you do it with me instead?"

"Technically it's 3 questions... And what the hell do you mean?" Vic was surprised and confused now.

Val saw it and smiled evilly. She slowed down, trying to find out if he was serious or just pretending. She realized her power over him, it was her moment of glory.

"I am not a doll, Vic, I have feelings. I know when a guy f*cks you, thinking about another woman. I had it before... But not with you. I hate it when guys are in love with someone else." For a moment Val became vulnerable, sad memories appeared in her mind. But she got it back in a second. "So, do I know her?"

"I have no idea what you are talking about." Vic sounded as convincing as he could, but Val noticed a tone of doubt.

She finished getting dressed and slammed the front door on her way out.

Vic kept standing in the bedroom, it seemed like he finally found what was slipping away from him. Val was right about the other woman, but the image was even blurrier now.

• • • •

"What were you girls talking about?" Dave wanted to ask the question but waited until Sky jumped in the pool. He didn't want to talk in front of her.

"Do I look like I know?"

"Ace, please..."

"Remember I told you that my child is special?"

"Are you talking about that special ability?"

"That one that you promised to keep in secret until the day you die... Or..."

"You'll kill me... Yeah, it was hard to forget."

"So, when something goes wrong, Sky needs to fix it. Like when a person knows something he shouldn't." I looked at Dave with an evil smile. "I think there is this way of things that should be followed. I never had a full picture of it. It's complicated."

"Can she remove memories?"

I nodded, looking at Sky diving under water.

"She can, but it's painful."

"Yeah, I think if she tried it on me, I would feel it. Did she do it to me? Please tell me she didn't..."

"If she did, would you remember her secret?"

Dave smiled. I touched his cheek. His beard was messy after swimming, so I brushed it softly with my nails. He was handling our secret surprisingly well. He was not only my first boyfriend that Sky liked, but he was also the first one whom she trusted with it.

"And I was not talking about another person, they're feeling headache, like after a hangover. It's nothing, compared to what it's doing to her." I stared at my little mermaid again.

"That's why she was in her room? And her nose looked like she was..."

"Bleeding..."

"That's how you realized what happened? Have you seen it before?"

"She did it to me once. We were experimenting. Don't you judge me. I wanted to know more about her powers and there were few things in my life I wouldn't bother to forget."

Dave looked shocked, but he calmed his breath quickly as Sky was going out of the pool already. "It never gets boring with you two, isn't it?"

"Welcome to a family, boyfriend."

"I think it's time for girls to talk..." Dave kissed my hand and went in the direction of the pool.

Sky took his seat next to me. She reached for her phone as we both needed Sue now.

I started asking: "Are you feeling OK?"

"I had better days." Sue sounded too positive for this phrase.

Sky continued typing "It was a guy. I met him on the bridge. He made me feel so angry. And you know when I'm angry, I can do it accidentally sometimes... I read him. But, I guess, it went wrong somewhere. I carved myself in his mind, I made him see me, us... I don't know. It's weird. It felt like we had a future together, but it shouldn't start now... It shouldn't click yet. But my anger forced it. I violated his present." She looked worried, keeping her eyes on the screen, struggling to find the words to express this weird scenario.

"What you're trying to say is... You made him fall in love with you earlier than he should?" It sounded crazy even for us.

Sky nodded. "But it's so wrong, I shouldn't just walk around and make people fall in love. I'm not a Cupid. It's against rules... So, I believe I was punished in an ironic way. When I said it went wrong, I didn't mean with him, I meant myself. It kind of backfired..." Sky was barely holding tears.

"What do you mean by that?"

"What I did to him, it slipped. It backfired on me. I fell in love with him."

"That explains tears... But if you both feel like this, can't you just leave it? Maybe it's your fate..."

"I cannot make a fate for myself." Sky smiled like it was something obvious and she was surprised why I didn't know that.

"So, you forced yourself out of his mind?"

"I had to. But it was harder than before, he was sort of fighting it, not letting me go... And it was too far, I never did it at such a distance... And he was with another woman... The only thing that helped was that he was drunk." Sky started sobbing.

I hugged her and kissed her hair. Dave was looking at us from the swimming pool, sad and admiring at the same time.

"So, what will you do now?"

Sky hesitated. "I will try to avoid him, to forget about him."

"Sounds like a plan."

"I wanted to thank you for giving me space."

"I had serious doubts about it..."

"And one more thing. Dave loves you."

"How dare you? How dare you read my boyfriend's mind? I thought we had rules about it. Weren't you punished enough, you evil little witch?" I started laughing and hit Sky with the pillow. "Do you think it's normal that you are telling me this before he did it himself? I will never forgive you, little sneaky..."

Sky started laughing, protecting her face from the pillow attack.

"This is a pure violation of privacy. This is war!"

She ran to the back door, I threw a pillow in that direction, hitting the hanging lantern. She was so adult and such a child in a way.

Dave looked even more confused now. I stood up from the sun lounge and went to him.

The water felt cold because my skin was probably burned with the sun already. I was always joking that I had two stages of suntan: very pale or completely burned, never in between. He watched me going down the ladder in the pool. I was not gracious, almost slipped and fell, but he was ready to catch me, always there for me. I put my palms on his shoulders, kissing him in the most sensitive way.

"What did she tell you?"

"She told me that you love me."

"I... Was asking about the memory loss story..."

"Ah, it looks like they fell in love, but she can't let it happen..."

"I feel lucky now."

"Why?"

"Because I managed to fall in love, and no one is erasing it from my memory."

"Let her just try to."

"I just told you that I love you, didn't I?"

"I don't remember..."

He shut my mouth with his lips. I pushed him away, angrily.

"Don't you want to know if I love you too?"

"No."

He kissed me repeatedly until I stopped fighting. I felt happy and guilty at the same time. My daughter was heartbroken, but I knew that one day she would allow herself to be in love, like I was now.

• • • •

"Whoever you are, I kind of hate you right now! Nothing personal, I hate everyone at 7am!" I knew that person behind the front door didn't hear me complaining while I was going down the stairs.

I rubbed my eyes, really needing to see the one who dared to ring the doorbell at 7am on my day off with my clearest vision. It would not feel that bad if I didn't fall asleep around 4am. Sky arrived home late yesterday and for most of the night we were busy chatting, gossiping, sharing. I took a second to replay it in my head, the moment when I hugged her for the first time in months. She had never been away from home for so long before.

I heard a doorbell again. Apparently, the person behind the door insisted on being killed. I opened it, but didn't see the face, it was hidden behind the huge bouquet of red roses. My heart stopped, as I realized that it was probably a dream, as it could not be real. I closed my eyes tight trying to wake up, but I was still standing, not sleeping.

His voice made me open my eyes: "Happy Birthday, Ace".

This voice was deep and charming, with worried notes... not like the other one. For many years, the first thing I saw on my birthday morning was my father, standing in the doorway with red roses. It was our thing. No matter where he was during the year, no matter how far, he would always come like this and greet me first. And he was traveling a lot, working in different countries, especially after divorce. But every year he was there for me, no matter what. He liked to say that there is nothing more important for him than me. Probably it was his way of expressing it, by being here for me on my special day.

I felt tears sliding down my cheeks. This was the first time since I remember myself when he couldn't make it, he died almost a year ago. Instead of my father, I was looking at a tall guy in a long black coat. His hair was shaved on the sides and pulled in a small ponytail on the back of his head. The look in his eyes was soft and caring.

I made wrong choices in my life, but this was a moment when I realized that most of my time I was with the best guys. Dave, my father, my brother Ben...

"How did you...?"

He was not waiting for me to form a proper question: "He made me promise that if something happens to him, I will take care of his girls…"

I couldn't stop my tears. Now I knew why Ben moved back to his house. One of the reasons, the official one, was that he wanted to come home and settle after many years of working abroad. But apparently, there was one more reason for it.

"I hate you."

"I love you too, Sis. And how about now?" I noticed that he was holding a cup of coffee in his hand.

"You look better now, but you're still the guy that woke me up at 7am on my day off. Is it even legal?" I enjoyed referring to him regarding law. The fact that he was one of the good guys, solving crimes and making this world a safer place was impressive. No one else I knew was brave enough to do it and I was extremely proud of his career.

"I thought you were coming for dinner tonight." I was still sleepy, but I remembered the plans we had, the party I spontaneously planned when I realized that both Sky and Ben will be around this day. The idea of spending my day in bed was tempting, but at least now I had someone to celebrate my birthday with. I really needed to chase away that overwhelming father grieving. The idea of Ben not being able to make it felt like sand slipping through my fingers while I was desperately trying to build a sandcastle right next to approaching waves.

But it still felt so solid. Me, step away from crying my eyes out, feeling so sad about losing a parent so early in life, Sky and Ben showing up right in the moment when I needed them, Dave knowing exactly how hard he needs to push me to keep moving without shattering me. I was feeling so fragile. They all were here for me now and I knew that they would not let me fall even if I did my best to perform as the toughest person on Earth.

People who didn't know me well never noticed this shift. At work I was still a solid boss, at home I was a cheerful girlfriend and caring mother... People who knew me well knew that there was a crying little girl covered in blankets and detached from reality hiding under that perfect impression. They all knew it, but didn't ask, didn't push, simply giving me the time and space I needed. I would come back from the grief bubble. I was strong enough to rip it apart and they believed in me. It felt like everyone was playing their role, knowing exactly what they needed to do. Just now Ben showed up with this symbolic rose tradition, knowing that it will put another brick in my new mental foundation.

"Oh, talking about that. Will it be pure family style, or can I bring someone?"

"Do you have someone on your mind? Go for it. I invited a few friends, and so did Dave. We'll make it a party style this year..."

"Should I eat at home?"

"No worries, Honey, I will not cook this time."

Ben smiled. He never lost an opportunity to tease me about my cooking failures.

"So, whom will you bring with you?" I tried to sound casual and not pushy, but curiosity was overwhelming. Ben never introduced me to any of his girlfriends. He always said that none of them are important enough, which sounded disturbing. There was a period when I was wondering if he is even straight. Not like it mattered. I didn't care about who he was attracted to. He couldn't find a bond with anyone, and I really wanted him to. Ben was much younger than me and still had all the time in the world, but the idea of life unpredictability was flowing over me for months now and I was holding myself back from a genuine desire to force it...

"There is one guy at work..."

I believe I accidentally slipped one of these "Oh, really?" looks, because he smiled understanding what I was thinking about.

"There is one guy at work. He's new in the department, he was transferred recently. He is kind of a jerk, thinking he is better than everyone... having trouble adjusting to the team..."

"So sweet, brother, you finally found a friend!" I think it sounded too ironic. I just tried to hide the disappointment of Ben not actually being romantic about the person he was inviting to my party.

"We are not friends. I just want to help him. I know how it feels to adapt to new surroundings. Been there, done that..." He absolutely did and I knew that. For most of his adult life, Ben always needed to prove himself. Being young, handsome and rich never made it easier for him. It was a challenge for my introvertive brother to step out of his comfort zone and prove how smart and talented he was, to prove that his candidacy was worth receiving a promotion, even though he was the least experienced out of all competitors. We were so similar in this...

"You don't need to explain. I just hope he will not make drama and fight with someone here."

"We're safe if Sky doesn't see him." Ben laughed at his own joke as it was not funny to me. I never forgave him for the party in his house, where he invited my 14-year-old daughter, and she ended up punching someone.

"You are not making things better by reminding me, Ben."

"Come on! It was 5 years ago and you're still angry?"

"Wait, let me check... Hell, yes!"

"How many times can I apologize?"

I shrugged. We both knew that I was not angry anymore, but I didn't like the way he reminded me about it. It was still surprisingly sharp in my mind.

"Anyway, she is not even here..."

"Who told you that?"

Ben and I both turned around because this voice was new to both of us. I haven't gotten used to the new Sue sound yet. She didn't sound like a GPS anymore, voice was softer and more natural, sounding like an actual human being now. Sky did an amazing job with the programming team. Sue now had different emotions, and her voice was adjusting according to the context, which proved the progress technologies reached in only a couple of years. She sounded like she knew what she was talking about now. New Sue's voice suited my daughter so much better.

Sky was standing in a living room behind our backs. One earphone in her ear, another one in her hand. I believe she was listening to us for a while now, enjoying the way I pretended to be angry at Ben.

Apparently, she was planning to jog as she had a sports top and leggings on. Her long silver hair was pulled up in a tight ponytail, her skin was tanned, her toned body didn't have a skinny teenage look anymore, it was so very fit now. I caught myself admiring her abs. My girl didn't look like a child anymore, she looked so adult now.

Ben hasn't seen Sky for a while. It was funny how life was spreading them all over the world, playing with the timings, like waiting for a moment when they would miss each other. When I saw it now, it all made sense. Sky was smiling so openly and widely; her eyes were shining. Ben was... shocked... I think he had a hard time recognizing her. But only for a moment. He stood up from the couch and was holding her in his arms after a moment. I saw her feet detaching from the ground as Ben was much taller and she was literally hanging on his neck now.

One tiny thought appeared in my mind at that moment, but I didn't know what it meant. I knew Ben all his life, but now something unfamiliar in him showed up. I wondered what it was...

• • • •

"Did I tell you how beautiful you look?"

I was standing in front of a mirror, putting on my new earrings. Dave was sitting on the bed and looking at my reflection.

"Last time you said it I was not dressed yet."

"I like you better that way..."

"What are you trying to say? Should I not wear a dress tonight?"

"Nooo, not that. Only I can enjoy the naked look."

"Let's see..."

I heard Sue's voice from behind the door: "Mother, I believe you're late for your own party. Guests started to arrive."

I heard one more doorbell. Without waiting for my answer Sky rushed downstairs to open it. I still had a couple of minutes before she came back to my door again to remind me that I was the host, not her. I looked at Dave and I knew that despite the obvious admiration, he was concerned. He saw the cracks in my surface and knew how well I played the game of hiding those. I was not trying to fool him, didn't even know if I could. He knew me better than I did myself, that's how it felt at least. I nodded quietly, just answering the unspoken question of his. Yes, I was alright and yes, I was ready to do it.

Sky rushed to the door once again, frustrated with the idea of how unfamiliar she was with the people coming to the house. She was feeling guilty for not being involved in my personal life. But this time it was someone she knew, it was Ben and the words just slipped as he couldn't help but notice how beautiful she looked: "Boy, you look stunning, small one. Whom are you trying to charm today?"

"Well, let's see. How about Dave's boss? Just look at him. We'll match perfectly together. His hair is also gray, same as mine." They giggled.

"Little devil…"

Sky wanted to close the door once Ben entered, but he stopped her. "Just wait for my guest, parking challenge."

"Let me guess! Tall, dark and beautiful? Looking like a model, thinking of becoming a 'Miss Universe', confident that beauty will save the world?" She knew his type better than I did.

Sky noticed Ben's confusion, but continued teasing him: "No? Having more than one thought at a time and being blond? Since when you're into blondes?"

"Since I met you." He smiled, but it didn't sound the way Ben expected, it felt awkward. He tried to change the subject, seeing that his guest was next to him already.

"Sky, this is Vic. We work together. Vic, meet my niece."

• • • •

"I brought you a coat." Ben needed to say something to notify her of his presence.

Sky was sitting on the bench in the backyard. Her eyes closed and legs crossed, meditating. Ben hated to disturb her, but looking at her in a short dress in the middle of winter outside was bothering him.

"But probably you don't need it and I'm just disturbing you… I'll just go…"

Sky shook her head and slapped a palm on the bench next to her, offering him a seat. She reached for her phone but realized that its battery died. It was a long day, lots of people to talk to. Sky showed Ben a black phone screen, gesturing to him that further communication might be challenging.

"I don't have mine on me either…" Ben just realized that he brought Sky a coat but was not wearing his own. The phone was probably in his pocket.

He tried to avoid using the phone during family gatherings, convincing himself that family is more important than work. Unfortunately, even the forgotten phone was not helping, his colleagues could find him anywhere… Detectives, what to say. During these moments when he needed to take off from birthday parties and family celebrations, Ben felt guilty and sorry that his guys were doing such an excellent job finding him.

Sky put phone back on the bench and hid her ice-cold hands in the coat pockets. She forgot the last time she was talking to someone without her phone, she smiled remembering a small notepad and a pen she was always carrying around as a child. Now she always had her phone instead, but it served as a barrier. It was hard to catch all the expressions of the person when you're typing all the time. It was hard without reading them. But it was easier in the way, conversation didn't feel so personal. She could talk to someone mostly without looking in their eyes and she did it most of the time. But what she was doing now, looking at Ben, felt personal.

"You can do it. You can make me believe that you're talking. I know that you don't like it because it's a lie. But when I know that it's fake, you're not lying to me."

Sky was surprised that he offered it. Last time she did it to Ben was at that famous party when he was pulling her away from the guy she punched. He was asking her something, but she was so angry and stressed, her adrenaline was high, she didn't have time to type, she just entered his mind and left her answer there. The feeling that followed was amazing. She calmed down, but the other emotions were overwhelming. It felt so personal, Ben was the only one in the crowd who heard her, heard her real voice, no one did before... It felt oddly satisfying just to be heard, even in this scenario, even without actually talking.

"Or I can just get you a power bank" Ben was looking for options as she was hesitating. He didn't know why, but he wanted that feeling again, feeling of Sky trusting him her voice.

"You know it's not safe, right?"

"Do you need my written agreement on this?"

"I'll try not to damage your brain..."

"If I let anyone mess with it, it should be you."

They smiled at each other. It was going well so far. Ben noticed that Sky didn't sound like Sue at all, her voice was softer and deeper. It was enjoyable, one of those voices that you want to hear all the time, calm and soft, satisfying.

"I actually just wanted to ask, what's wrong with you?"

Sky didn't answer. It depended on what he knew...

"You're sitting here alone, while all that crowd is leaving and asking your mother to say 'goodbye' to you."

"I just need to put my shit together." Sky smiled realizing she didn't put her words through a regular filter. She usually did it while typing, but now, it was pure thoughts, pure her.

"Hmm... I thought you never lost your shit..." Her sad smile followed, and he understood how wrong he was now. "Or wait, I remember the day years ago, you spent locked in your room. Ace called me when I was in the bar with the guys. She said it was bad."

Sky was surprised that he remembered. Was it the first and only time she lost it? Why did he keep this memory specifically, while for all these years she was working on forgetting it? Why did he remember it now when she once again was affected by the same issue?

It was hard to filter her own thoughts with the words she was transmitting to Ben.

"Hard time being a teenager." Now she was desperately hiding real emotions behind an ironic smile.

Ben shook his head. "Something happened during the party today, making you lose it. What was it?"

"It was the guy, who was the reason for my hiding in the room. And you were the one who brought him here". She was shocked. How easy it came out, how judgmental it sounded. She didn't mean it this way, or maybe she did. Deep inside Sky knew that it was not Ben's fault, but it felt so much easier to make it his responsibility.

"No way... This world is so freaking small... I'm so sorry, Honey, I didn't know..."

"You couldn't know." At least it sounded true.

"Do you hate me?"

"I do..." All her emotions were in this short answer. She felt Ben flinching, getting hurt for a split second.

Sky suddenly felt nauseous, she turned away from Ben, breaking the connection. He touched her shoulder, and it felt like an electrical shock. Her body was shaking, but not from cold this time.

"It cannot be the last thing you tell me." Ben moved closer and hugged her from behind.

Sky turned back to him, feeling the cold of his palms with her hands, realizing that now he was the one getting cold. She opened her coat, letting him in, covering Ben with it as much as she could with the limited fabric. She felt his cold touch on her lower back, his chest with her cheek, his heartbeat, noticing that it was too quick. She couldn't stop feeling him, needing more, diving into his thoughts.

It was shocking, but she knew it was not a mistake. She punched her fists in his breast and pushed him away, maintaining just enough distance to look into his eyes.

"I hate you, Ben."

"No, you don't. You're not the only one here who can read people, Sky."

"I am."

"You can say as much as you want, but I know what you're thinking now." He watched his hand touching her chin, cheek, putting the small wild hair lock behind her ear. He smiled thinking how this curly lock was reflecting her nature right now, willing to go out of a tight ponytail, like it was fighting with the internal rules and mindset.

He felt her fists on his chest becoming softer, her cold fingers sliding up his neck. Ben pulled Sky closer to him. He wanted to say something to break the silence, but he couldn't find words that would not push her away, scare her off. It was a fringe and there were two choices: jump to the unknown dark hole in the ground or go back. He had only one chance to make it right.

"Read me..."

Sky looked up at him again and closed her eyes, wanting it more than she thought. For a couple of long seconds, she was breathing as deeply as it was possible, not having enough air in her lungs. She was not only reading, but she was also feeling him, like she never did before. She was never so intimately close to anyone. All her past relationships became a black and white photo on the backside of her mind, this was different, this was new. She made the distance between their faces as short as it was possible now. For a second, she felt his hesitation, but it was gone in a moment, like a tiny boat covered by the mighty ocean wave.

Her lips felt cold and the desire to make them warm again was unstoppable.

Devil on his shoulder was repeating to Ben: "She read you, she felt you, she wants it as much as you want... It feels so good, so right..."

Angel on the other side was almost screaming: "Are you f*cking kidding me? It cannot happen! She is your niece. Stop kissing her, she is your family!"

Ben didn't listen to any of them, he couldn't. The sound of him kissing her, the sound of her breath, the sound of her hands touching his face... it was more than he could hear now, he was absorbed with it, not needing anything else in the world.

Sky couldn't find the border between his overwhelming feelings and hers. She couldn't stop him; she couldn't stop herself. Feeling his lips on hers, on her neck, feeling his hands pulling her closer and closer to him. It was like nothing she knew before.

• • • •

Vic was sitting behind his desk, staring at the pile of papers almost covering him from other people in the room. Probably new colleagues decided to punish his temper by pushing all this paperwork to his desk.

He thought that he was proving his power and leadership qualities, but apparently it went wrong somewhere. His new colleagues didn't bend, didn't follow his guide as people usually did. They had a stronger leader here and they just dismissed Vic, labeling him a cocky new guy. Teamwork will not be a part of his resume when the new boss decides to get rid of him, probably by transferring him. But things could still get better, Vic just needed a chance... He was moved here because of a fight he started with one jerk in his previous precinct. He will not do it here; he could not afford to be that stupid again.

It was because of Val. Even after all those years it was still Val, his ongoing curse. Four years ago, she finally disappeared from his life. He heard that she found a guy, got married, and had a big house with a dog in the yard. Tom was telling him everything in detail as she chose not to lose connection with him at least. Vic expected not to see her again and was relieved that she found her peace.

But one rainy day she stepped into his precinct looking for him. Val knew where he was, she knew where to find him even after losing sight of him for years. Or did she? Was she still getting updates about his life? Was Tom sharing Vic's life news with her? Probably... Vic never asked him not to.

Vic never saw Val like this. She had a black eye, scratches and wounds all over her body, but she was holding on with a straight posture, pretending that she was fine, playing a role she played in public: strong and confident no matter what. In the next half an hour she told him everything about her unsuccessful marriage and abuse, she wanted to file a report. That was the moment when one of Vic's now ex colleagues commented: "What did you expect from your husband if you were dressing like a hooker?". It was correct in the way, Val always showed her body more than a woman should in public, especially a married woman. Vic knew that and agreed with the jerk's opinion deep inside, but it was Val sitting in front of him with her husband's blood under her fingernails. It was the same Val that got hurt so many times, even if it was not physical. He did hurt her and regretted it now, he owed her this one and she was calling for this favor now. This was the moment when Vic lost it and punched the guy. Once, twice, he couldn't even recall how many times because his mind was filled with instincts, anger. He was fighting a bully, like he always did, he was protecting his person, not even realizing until then that Val was his friend.

And now he was sitting behind his new desk in the new precinct, thinking where he should run away in the evening, because Val stayed in his apartment now. He offered it as she didn't have many options and he would feel much better, knowing that she is under his protection in case her husband comes looking for her. He was not sure if she needed it, but she took the offer and there was no way back now, even though he would happily take it back. Even worse, shortly after, he realized that being there for her meant giving Val hope. It looked like she still didn't get over that crush she had on him and now he was her savior, a man who now should take care of her, the one she was always wanting as a fragile little girl dreaming of a prince... But it was not a fairy tale and Vic just wanted to rip this dream apart, go out, get drunk, pick up a girl, bring her home and close the question about him and Val forever. He was pathetic and he knew it. But that's how he sorted his issues before. Brutal, rough, there was no space for discussions and conversations, only actions. That was exactly what attracted so many women to him, exactly what made Val fly in his direction even if he was burning her wings. It was his nature, the only way he knew how to operate.

How surprised he was when Ben came by with a wide smile, offering him to fetch a few drinks after work, casually mentioning that his sister is having a birthday party tonight and the bar there will be good, making a casual note that he can't promise the same about the food. Vic didn't even realize how he agreed. It could be his chance to fix the damaged relationships in his department, his chance to run away from whatever was happening between him and Val, it was the lemon given to him by almost a stranger and he was definitely going to use it to make a lemonade.

The funniest part was that he remembered Ben. Long before he started working here. He was Val's 'cutie in black' from the bar, he was the guy she was trying to charm that night. What were the chances that for the second time, even without knowing Val, Ben was saving Vic from her.

Vic was thinking about it while parking his car next to Ben's sister's house. He saw Ben talking to someone in a doorway. It was his last chance to drop this ridiculous idea of coming to a party, turn his car around and just go. But he felt that he was not ready to give up on this lemon.

So now he was on the threshold and saw Sky. For a few seconds he was stunned by her beauty. Undoubtedly, she was the most beautiful woman he ever saw. It felt weird and she looked familiar, but he didn't remember meeting her in the past as he would definitely remember that. The memory was flowing in his mind, but he was not able to catch it, like a dream slipping away the moment you opened your eyes. The plan about hooking up with someone and bringing her home in front of Val felt more appealing now.

Ben introduced them and the small one appeared to be his niece. Deep inside Vic was swearing at Ben for having such a stunning relative. She was communicating in a weird way, didn't talk but apparently heard them. That was so f*cking familiar... Vic was trying to tighten a grip on this memory, forcing it back in his mind, but it was all liquid, just streaming through his fingers. The girl obviously didn't recognize him, so probably he was just imagining it. Probably they have never met before...

The evening was pleasant, Ben's sister appeared to be very sweet and friendly. Surprisingly, Sky looked nothing like her mother or father, only gestures and facial expressions were similar. It planted a seed in Vic's mind, but he didn't bother to watch it sprouting.

He decided not to hit on Ben's niece, as it could spoil his relationships with the only friendly person in the new precinct. But throughout the party, despite the plan, many times he had an urge to look at her, to find her smiley face in a crowd, to talk to her... Which, surprisingly, never happened. The girl did a fantastic job avoiding him, being continuously busy with something... or involving herself in a conversation Vic didn't feel like being a part of. But he just couldn't find the excuse not to look at her, constantly stopping himself from doing it, realizing how creepy it might look.

By the end of the party, Ben came to him with the same friendly smile on his face: "I hope it was not too boring, man..."

"No, it was just what I needed. Thank you." He meant it. Being here completely erased all his worries.

"Not for thank you. When you decide to leave, just don't wait for me, I'll take a taxi or maybe even crash in a guest room."

"Sure, no problem." Deep inside Vic was still wondering why out of all the guys from work Ben invited him, but that was not a question he could ask.

Ben took the coat and went outside through the back door.

Something was different in this family. Vic couldn't silence his detective mind. Ace was funny and adorable, Dave friendly and interesting. They both had huge respect and support from every person in the crowd and it didn't feel fake. Apparently, most of the guests were coworkers as they were discussing restaurants all the time. Ben was admiring his sister and her family. It was obvious how much appreciation he had for moments like this. It was more important to him than work.

It felt weird to Vic, he didn't believe in tight family relationships, but looking at them gave him ideas he never had before. He imagined himself as a part of it, but shook it off, his nature rejecting it. Vic saw in this family something he wanted to see in his own family one day. Love, support, success... it felt so right to be around them, he felt like he was charging from them with positive energy.

Vic thought that he would be happy to have Ben in his friend circle. Maybe it was whiskey talking, but he wanted to offer Ben to continue drinking, maybe going to his place. Val was charmed by him once already, he could switch her attention again.

He took his coat and stepped out through the back door, assuming Ben was still there as he never came back. When Vic saw him, he realized what was wrong with this family, which seemed so normal just a moment ago.

Ben was sitting on the bench next to his niece and... kissing her. Vic froze, most of the whiskey he consumed until now evaporated during those short seconds. He couldn't believe his eyes.

His first idea was that Ben was forcing him on her, as he was holding her so tight, but then he realized it was mutual.

Sky was enjoying it, her eyes were closed, her face glowing with pleasure.

"That is just sick..." Vic didn't say it out loud, but it looked like Sky heard it, because she immediately opened her eyes and looked at him, like she knew exactly where he was standing. She slapped her fists into Ben's chest, and he turned around too.

Sky pushed Ben away and just ran inside the house, not even looking in Vic's direction. Ben stood up facing Vic, waiting for him to say something.

"I'm not here to judge you, but it is just so sick, man..." Vic whispered, feeling how their potential friendship was going down the drain.

"You don't understand." Ben was trying to catch his breath.

"Go ahead, explain to me why I just caught you kissing your niece. Or is it not what I saw?"

"She is not my niece... she is, but... we aren't related, she was adopted."

"Oh, that's better... but still, you probably changed her diapers..."

"I didn't, and it's none of your business." Ben almost roared the last words, and Vic saw the fire in his eyes. Instead of a smiley friendly Ben, Vic finally saw the man, who was followed by the precinct without questions asked.

"Yes, you're right. I can't blame you, that girl is flaming hot..." He took a step back, knowing what he might trigger.

"Shut up!"

Vic was hurting Ben, he felt it in his voice, in his posture, in his eyes. Ben was raging, but he looked more confused than Vic was at the moment. It was not planned. It had never happened before. Vic sensed it. He saw the shift in the way Ben looked at Sky in the beginning of this party and the way he stared at the back door now, reevaluating, thinking, planning.

"I'll just go... see you at work." Vic retrieved and Ben just kept standing next to the bench. He turned his head and saw Sky's phone there.

"Damn it, Sky..." He mumbled.

• • • •

"Let me in... Please." Ben knocked at her door softly. He pressed his forehead against it, trying to feel what was on the other side.

Sky appeared in a doorway, her hair loose, her feet bare. She seemed even tinier without high heels, barely reaching his shoulder with the top of her head.

"Can I come in?"

It was a stupid question as the door was wide open. He obviously was invited.

"We need to talk."

Sky took her phone from his hand and connected it to the power bank. They were sitting in silence on her bed watching the phone coming back to life.

"Sky, I... I'm sorry."

"That is not what a girl wants to hear after she was kissed."

She smiled ironically. Sue's voice sounded so annoying now. Ben didn't want to hear it, but he didn't want to ask Sky to do her magic either... Not now at least.

"I cannot explain how it happened. I feel so ashamed and confused."

"One more thing that a girl doesn't want to hear."

"Sky..."

"Will you get in trouble?"

"Your mother will kill me. If she won't, Dave will hunt and torture me..."

"I'm not talking about them. I'm talking about Vic. He saw us... You're working together... I can't remove his memories... again." She looked puzzled, thinking of the way to save his reputation, to protect him.

"What are you talking about?"

"I did it to him before, one more time can be dangerous. I can try, but..." The idea of diving inside Vic's mind again was hurting her, like she was pressing on the wound which was not completely healed.

"Why do you want to remove his memories?"

"Because he saw us..." She cocked her head with surprise. How was he not getting it?

"I will talk to him. I explained to him already that we are not related... I'll explain again. God, it's confusing..."

"You're telling me... I was there."

"Wait... if you are planning memory loss for him... are you doing the same..."

"For you..."

Something inside of Ben was boiling now, he couldn't believe his ears. He took Sky's phone from her hands and threw it behind her on the pillow. He was angry as all the time she was typing, not looking in his eyes, hiding.

"Look at me."

Sky shook her head still staring at her hands where the phone was a few seconds ago. She felt weak.

"Look at me, Sky. Look me in the eyes and tell me that you wanted to remove from my head the happiest moment I had in years." He took her hand in his, it was still cold. He spread her fingers, gently touching all of them one by one, and put her palm on his heart.

Sky felt his heartbeat, her hand was shaking now, reflecting on the vibe underneath it. She looked up at him, turned away searching for her phone.

"No, no phones... Please talk to me."

"We talked enough... There, on the bench... one nice talk."

"Damn it, Sky. Stop pretending that you didn't feel anything."

"I was upset, you were comforting."

"Not like this... That's not what it was." At least he didn't want it to be true. He shook his head, trying to get rid of the idea that what he thought she felt was a lie, that it was just an accident...

"Look at me." He noticed that she was dropping her gaze again, she couldn't stand looking at him.

Beautiful gray eyes finally stared at him and now he could tell if she was lying. Those eyes never lied to him.

"You read me, you felt me..." He grunted.

Sky nodded. She knew where he was going with it.

"Tell me I was wrong thinking you felt the same at this moment."

Sky moved closer to him. Ben didn't expect that. She slid on her knees as close as she could.

"There is only one way to check if you felt what you felt, not what I made you feel."

"Do it. I want to know. Now. Stop playing these tricks, just do it."

Sky sat on the bed and crossed her legs. She felt the need to explain what she was doing: "I'll drop the connection. Whatever influence I might have on you, whatever charms I might use, I'll get rid of it, leaving it clean, like it is."

Ben was desperately serious: "Do what you feel is right."

He was overwhelmed with the idea that she put all this in his head, that it was just fake. That it was her creation... She really was so dangerous, playing with minds... But he couldn't complain, she warned him. After a minute of sitting cross-legged, she finally opened her eyes. It seemed like it worked. Ben felt mentally drained, his mind was blurry and clear at the same time.

Sky put her hand on his cheek, looking at him, like she wanted to ask something. After she touched him, Ben felt alive again. He slid his fingers through her silver hair. Sky closed her eyes, enjoying his touch. His hand moved to her neck, shoulder, waist. Second hand joined and he was holding her waist from both sides now. He put her up, like she didn't weigh anything at all and sat her on his lap. Weird feelings came through his body as he remembered her sitting like this when she was a child. Ben banished these thoughts as he didn't care now. All he knew now was the woman in front of him, all he wanted was her.

Her eyes were still closed, Sky felt his lips on her neck. She was burning from inside and when the moment came, his lips finally touched hers. So hot and so hungry. She was absorbed by him, overpowered, helpless. She bit his lip just to feel that it was real, he was real. He flinched for a second, but didn't let her go, and continued kissing her with more and more passion. Sky found her legs wrapped around his waist, she felt so close to him, and she didn't want to move back. But common sense appeared suddenly in her mind, and she pushed him away, moving as far from him as she could now. She took her phone from the pillow and started typing:

"Now we need to talk..."

Ben took a minute to think straight again, it was not as easy as it sounded. He looked at her angrily.

"Don't even think about taking it from me. I don't care if it's wrong, don't you dare to remove these memories from my mind."

"Ben... Don't you want to move on without knowing it happened?"

"That's your solution? Forget it? Why?"

"Because you're my uncle."

"I am. What's next? What other excuses do you have? What else will you pull out your sleeve? Any other reasons to reject me? Why are you making it so hard to reach you, Sky? You did your test, right? Tell me now if it's real? Tell me, Sky!"

"I didn't have any influence on you, I promise. It was real, same on the bench. It was not me." She sounded both relieved and upset now.

• • • •

Sky stepped out of the shower, pulling on pajamas. She was wondering if Ben was in her room still. She opened the door and looked at her bed. He was so emotionally drained that he just fell asleep, hugging her pillow. Sky came closer and looked at him judgingly. How could things change overnight? Only a few hours ago he was Uncle Ben, now he was a man who touched something important in her, something complicated and new.

"Ben..." He didn't show any signs of living, he was deeply asleep.

Struggling for a bit, she managed to pull a blanket from underneath his body and cover him with it instead. Then she turned the light off. This day was finally gone.

"Please, man, it's only for one week, ten days max." Seeing that Ben was not ready to agree, Vic added: "Maybe less... I just really want her to be safe."

"And why should I agree? Inviting the woman I never met before to live in my house?"

"Temporary..." Vic bit his tongue, trying not to remind Ben that he met Val before. There was a strong chance he didn't remember it.

"Not convincing. Doesn't she have any other friends to stay with?"

"Her other friends are not cops."

"So, you want her to stay with me because I'm a cop?"

"She will be safe with you."

"So, what you're trying to say is, the girl who filed a report against her husband and got you transferred from a precinct because you were fighting for her, is not safe... Are you trying to set me up for something?"

Vic grimaced, thinking how well Ben was reading his evil plan. Yes, he would not mind Ben and Val hooking up, but it was not a main reason for him asking Ben for this favor. He was worried that Val's husband would take advantage of him leaving town.

"Your house is like a freaking palace; you will not even see her. And Val is flaming hot... maybe you two can get along..."

Vic received exactly the reaction he expected. Now Ben was frustrated.

"Oh, really? You should be the last person hooking me up with someone, you're the only one who knows about me having a..." Ben hesitated, looking around, thinking of what would happen if his secret would be revealed.

"Girlfriend? When will you relax already? Sal was gossiping about you finding a new girl the next day after 'it' happened. Don't forget that you're surrounded by a bunch of detectives, some of them are capable of recognizing secrets."

Vic was right. Next day after the birthday party every single guy in the precinct was asking Ben what happened to him and why he looked so happy. And it happened despite him trying to hide his emotions. He was not a bad actor, but there were things he couldn't hide.

"Any plans to tell someone about the reason for your happy look?" Despite all the jokes he made already and all the teasing, Vic was happy for him... maybe even jealous a little.

"It's not that easy... We want to see if it works out first before shocking our relatives."

• • • •

Ben and Sky had 'the conversation', and it was a bit intense. That day they agreed not to tell anyone about what's happening. It was the day after the party. Ben was finally finding his way home after a day full of teasing by his colleagues. Vic made it even more complicated, letting guys know that he met Ben's mystery girl.

58

When he finally parked his car next to the house, Ben exhaled, visualizing all the awkward situations in precinct, grateful that this day finally came to end. He was extremely exhausted... until he saw her. Sky was sitting on his porch, holding her phone in her hand and staring at him, probably realizing how he felt.

They didn't talk in the morning because Ben overslept and was rushing to work. She was obviously here to sort it out. Perfect timing. It was Ben's butler off, so no one could bother them in his house.

Looking at her, Ben realized that just this morning he woke up next to her, hugging her pillow, inhaling the fruity smell of her hair, barely touching her. It felt different...

He didn't feel manly and powerful, looking at the naked women in his bed, instead he felt confused and defeated by Sky who was wearing pajamas with blue unicorns on it.

He didn't need to exchange numbers with her just in case one of them wanted to hook up again, he desperately wanted her to text him today, but she never did.

He didn't need to make up an excuse to get rid of girl if she wanted something bigger than one night stand. He needed an excuse to meet her.

He didn't feel the need to break relationships, he wanted to make it work for the first time in his life.

"Why didn't you come inside?" That was a stupid question to ask, but he tried to start casual conversation and sound polite.

"Tough day?"

Ben nodded. "How was yours?"

"Having a hard time explaining to your sister why you spend the night in my bed…"

Ben's expression changed at once. His muscles tensed. All his body was expressing a numb statement. He started to wonder why Ace never called him asking, what the hell happened… or even showed up at work frustrated…

"Not my best joke, I guess." Sky looked guilty, seeing how much stress she just made him experience. "Don't worry. They didn't notice anything. Thanks to overall hangover and rush to work."

Now it was Ben's turn to feel awkward, but he didn't, he was relieved: "You, little devil."

Sky smiled with her evil smile.

• • • •

"So…" Ben realized that he should start the conversation. He was trying to move his focus from water bubbles in his glass to Sky. Every time he looked at her, he felt like his skin was burning and the only thing that would save him was her healing touch, her skin, her hair, her breath… and he was back to watching bubbles again. It was really hard to concentrate when she was sitting next to him. He could reach her by spreading a hand, but he couldn't, not until they figured it out.

"So…" Sky couldn't stop staring at his face. His confused look, his willingness to hold his emotions together. All of this was a perfect addition to her overwhelming feelings. She was desperately holding herself from moving closer to him to feel his heat, his breath, his touch. Hell, all this was so weird.

"I think..." Ben finally managed to look into her eyes: "We shouldn't tell them yet. Not until we decide what to do about it."

"I just need to check something." Sky put her phone away and moved closer to Ben.

He lost all interest in bubbles and put his glass on the coffee table. There was nothing more important, there was no need to hold it together now. There was no alcohol in his blood anymore to make him more confident with her. But it didn't matter. His skin was burning, and it felt hotter because she was so close to him now. She wanted to check if it was real, he also wanted to know if what he felt yesterday was not a dream, not an illusion. There was a question they had to answer now.

In one second everything disappeared, all the doubts and worries. Sky was laying on her back, squeezed into a soft couch by the weight of Ben's body. He was acting without thinking, without plan, just taking what he desperately wanted. Her touch made him shiver, her lips made him hungry, he felt her cold hands touching his neck and slowly sliding under his t-shirt. He felt her tongue playing with his, her lips teasing him, giving him full access and then pulling back with a playful smile. He was absorbed by her, something he had never felt before. He felt desperate. Before, with other women, it was always under control. But here and now something just broke inside of him, he couldn't stop anymore. Ben knew Sky was feeling him, he knew that she lost control as well. They shared this overwhelming moment. Nothing else mattered.

• • • •

Ben realized that thinking about it for one more second would make him sit behind his desk for a while. He definitely needed an ice-cold shower now. He even forgot for this long moment of silence that Vic was still sitting in the chair next to his desk, waiting for a solution for Val's temporary relocation.

"You look like you're thinking about her." Vic became suspicious.

Despite how inappropriate it was right now, Ben couldn't stop visualizing undressing Sky on his couch, covering her with his body, making her breathe so heavily.

It was a week ago, but still felt so fresh. Ben tried his best to stop this daydreaming. He needed to get rid of Vic, this guy was reading him too good: "One week. You have one week."

"I didn't expect more." Vic smiled gloriously. "Thank you! You will not regret it. I promise."

Well, that wink was inappropriate. Now Ben had to find out how the woman he is charmed with will react to the news about another woman, apparently sexy as hell, moving in with him for a week. Damn, how did Vic trick him into this? Sky took Ben's guard down again and it was not a good timing.

He took his phone out of the pocket and started typing. It was better to tell her this now than to wait until she read it from his mind. Ben smiled as it sounded weird. Sky never read him without permission, but he remembered one time when she lost control. It felt like in the moments of overwhelming passion, she couldn't see the difference between his and her emotion, so it all became hers. He was kind of jealous that she could actually feel double of what he felt. Ben stopped himself from thinking about it because the memories of that day made his skin boiling hot again. This little devil was more than he could imagine, more than he was ever handling, she stole his mind.

Ben resumed typing: "Hey. Busy?"

He received a message back almost at once: "Hi, just getting ready for a meeting. Do you want to see me in the evening?"

She was asking. Of course, he wanted, with every single body cell. Ben looked at a bunch of paperwork covering most of his table. He was delaying it for a week already, now it was time to work and give his devil time to miss him a bit.

"Can't. Need to work before I get fired for all this unfinished paperwork."

"Can they fire you? I thought you're a big boss..."

"Don't push..." One more word and Ben would close his eyes pretending not to see all these folders and run to see her in the evening.

"I never do it, Babe. Always your choice." Following this message, she sent him a photo of her reflection in the mirror. "What do you think?"

Did he really need to answer that? Ben felt his skin becoming flaming hot again. She was wearing a short and a bit tight black dress, high heels... Silver hair was wavy and messy, covering her bare shoulders. Ben felt a wave of jealousy crushing into his mind.

"Where did you say you're going?" He tried to sound as casual as possible.

"I didn't say. Just a small meeting with my ex. He messaged me today, wanting to meet."

"In that dress?" Ben tried his best to stop his own fingers from typing that.

A short pause followed, it felt like Sky didn't know what to say. Ben slapped his forehead with his palm, thinking how stupid he was, talking to her like this, like a jealous guy. Ben never felt jealous before, he didn't care that much. He didn't need to bother. It offended many of his girlfriends. Some of them even tried to make him feel jealous, but he was calm as always, saying something like "If you like him that much, go, get him." Not even one of his girls made him feel like he felt during those seconds of Sky's silence. Where did old Ben go?

"Yep."

"Great. Text me when you are going to be free. I have weird news."

"Ok. Talk later. Have fun with your paperwork."

"You too. Have fun."

The last words were scratching Ben's throat. Good that they were not talking, he probably couldn't pronounce it without judging or jealous notes in his voice. Ben put his phone aside and stared at the pile of papers, thinking about that black dress and how he wanted her to look like this only for him.

• • • •

"I think he's jealous" Sky was typing it with an evil smile, excitedly biting her bottom lip.

"Can you blame him? Did you look in the mirror today?"

Max paused, staring at Sky.

He couldn't believe that she was his once, and now she was telling him about secretly dating her uncle. It was weird, but, surprisingly, he could process it, like anything else... Whatever kept her next to him. The friendly lunch dates they had were ridiculous, but he still needed them, desperately. It couldn't get romantic between them, not anymore, but he couldn't afford to lose her. Max still loved her with all his heart. Unfortunately, it was not enough for both of them.

They tried. That's how you can describe their relationships. They tried for a few months, having romantic dates, holding hands, convincing each other how good it felt to become a couple after years of friendship. They tried to pretend that it could work out. It didn't... Max had a constant feeling of not being able to reach her. It felt like he was trying to own her, but he didn't have enough power to tame this little devil. She was close to him, but not within his reach.

Anyway, he was grateful for the effort. Despite all the weirdness of those relationships, it felt more real than the ones he had now.

"Is she jealous?" Sky tilted her head, expressing something similar to concern.

"Do you really want to know? I'm not even sure I should tell her that we met... you know how she feels about you..."

Probably he shouldn't blame her. And... Yes, terribly jealous! Once he was showing Mel old photos and one of them had Sky on it. He was stupid not deleting this one, he was too weak to do it. The photo had one precious moment, one of those memories he wanted to keep forever. On that photo Sky was looking at him, laughing at something. From a certain perspective, it could look like she was in love with him. It could seem this way if you didn't know the truth. That's why he never was able to delete it. How could he? Even if it was not real, it was a precious moment, it was his dream.

That look on Mel's face though... Dear God! It seemed like for the split second she felt jealous, angry, weak, uncomfortable, unconfident and all this was covered with a badly played careless smile and a single word: "Pretty..." This word was the only truth she was not able to hide.

Should he tell her that he was meeting Sky regularly? Should he tell her that Sky is dating now? ... if you can call it that. He loved Mel and he couldn't understand what was better in this case: hurt her by telling the truth or hurt her by lying about it.

"Should I tell her?"

"I'm not a good advisor..."

"Are you ever getting jealous?"

A small flashback appeared in Sky's memories. Memory of Val and Vic, one of those memories she was trying to erase for years. How stupid it was to be jealous of a guy that was not even hers?

"I was... long ago. Was young and stupid."

"And now when you are old and experienced... Will you be jealous of Ben?"

"I'm not a snow queen, I have feelings." She dropped it with a surprisingly cold expression.

"But you can control them better..."

"I mostly keep my shit together."

"Said the girl dating her uncle."

"You are a terrible, terrible friend!"

"And you are a devil..."

"That's weird... Ben also calls me that..."

Sky smiled mysteriously. The picture of Val was still in her head because of a reason. She felt something was going to happen involving her. Something challenging.

"How are you hiding the truth from your parents?"

"I'm not 'TELLING' them anything." Sky laughed. Sue pronounced the highlighted word exceptionally loud, so the guy on the nearest table looked at her suspiciously.

"Oh, really. You're pulling this joke now?"

"Ace is not asking yet. She's quite busy and giving me more space, probably still getting used to the idea that I'm back."

"How about Dave?"

"Let me see. Last time I talked to him about my personal life was... Oh, I know, never!"

"Lucky you. My parents are squeezing my throat expecting to meet Mel."

"It was your choice to tell them about her..."

"Don't put it on me, lady! You should see mom's look when she starts this conversation about grandchildren. I had a choice: to adopt a child at once or to give her at least the name of a girl I'm dating, so she will stop asking me about..."

"Me..." She knew, she understood. "By the way, if you feel like adopting a child, I know a place..."

Max threw a tissue he was stressfully crumbling in his hand for a while now, in the direction of Sky's face. It never reached its destination because of its light weight, but he was satisfied. The guy on the nearest table looked weird at them again.

"So, when are you going to tell him?" Max gained an evil shine in his eyes.

"About?"

"About the trip."

"Well. That's how you're changing the subject. Neatly done, man!" Sky stopped typing. Her eyes reflected multiple emotions. She looked like a child intrigued with a new toy, not understanding yet if she liked it, or hated it, or even feared it.

"If you want to drop it, now it's the right time to tell me…"

"Why on earth do you think I want to drop it?"

"Sometimes it feels like I want it more than you."

"Actually, it was your idea…"

"Like anyone can convince you to do something you're not into!!! Come on, woman! Whom are you trying to fool here?"

"Sometimes I forget how well you know me." Sky smiled softly. The same kind of smile was on her face when Max offered her to start dating. Same soft smile.

"When will you tell Mel?"

"When I'm sure that she is in a proper mood… when stars align… and when I stop believing that our relationships will not survive this."

"Or you can tell her when we have dates confirmed. She can even go with us…"

"Oh, really, Sky!? Why didn't I think about it?" Max was faking enthusiasm with fantastic energetic acting. "Mel, Babe. I'm going away with Sky for a month or two. I will probably be terribly busy, so I'll not be able to talk to you often. But if you feel like it, you can drop your work and your life and travel with us. What do you think?"

"I would watch that movie."

"You're evil… Oh wait! Coming soon…" Max cleared his throat, putting his fist to his mouth. "Dear Ben, I know we just started … whatever it is… But I'm going away with my ex for a few months. It will be only me and him traveling through the country, side by side. Oh, no, please don't be jealous."

"Let's see, whose relationships will survive that."

• • • •

"You wanted to tell me something." Sky was out of the shower, wearing gray striped pajamas, her hair was wet.

Ben was delaying this conversation as much as he could. He was sitting on the couch, the one that was holding those amazing memories of him and Sky. This time he was not staring at bubbles in his water glass, he was staring at ice cubes in his bourbon glass. He tried to sound as casual as it was possible... if you even can sound like something through texts.

"Vic has a friend..."

Sky smiled. Finally, this puzzle was completed. She was wondering all day why Val's image stuck in her mind. Now she understood.

"Apparently, she has a challenging life. He asked me to take care of her while he is away."

Sky smiled even wider but didn't text anything. Ben put it nicely. Probably he practiced this conversation in his mind a few times.

"I hope you don't mind her staying in my house."

Sky paused, barely holding her laugh. It was late and she didn't want to wake her parents up.

"Sure, as far as you're ok with that."

Ben was staring at his phone screen. She didn't care, at least it looked like it. This girl was something different...

"Will you allow her in your bed if she is scared to sleep alone?"

69

"Only if you are not there." Ben was picking up the rules of her game.

"I will not stand in the way of your happiness."

"No worries, I'll have time for both of you."

That sounded harsh, Ben regretted sending this message, squeezing glass in his hand, hoping it will not crush, hoping she will not take it seriously.

"I think I forgot to mention that I'm not into this... sharing a man is not for me... But you're free to enjoy it."

Ben felt his heart skipping a beat or two. She was not joking this time and it was hurting him. They never finished discussing their relationships, never called themselves a couple, never settled, never talked about how exclusive this is or will be. A terrible thought came to his mind. He never told her that he wants to be the only man, that he is not into this free relationship thing, not anymore. Starting from now, starting with her. A million thoughts appeared in his mind, jealous and stupid. Realizing that he didn't reply, he quickly started typing.

"I know that it's not yet clear and not quite official between us, Sky. But I want it to be exclusive, no casual dating drama. Don't even think about it."

"I'll consider your offer, Ben. Time to sleep. Good night."

She was holding her phone, with a smile. On the other side of the city, he was holding his phone in confusion.

• • • •

Sky couldn't fall asleep that night, thoughts invading her mind. Lots of things bothered her. She was happy to hear that Ben is interested in exclusive relationships. It was not typical for him. She was just wondering what had changed. Sky knew that she was different but was it enough to change the lifestyle of this guy? He had many girlfriends of sorts, all pretty, some of them even smart enough to understand what kind of relationships he needed. And now he wanted something new.

And she was also wondering if this time she would feel different. Since Vic happened in her life she was in all kinds of relationships with different guys, but she never loved them, she never pronounced these words even if they did it, looking at her, desperately waiting for an answer. She was still young, but it was not an excuse, not in her case. She was too different to believe that she was normal.

Once she was sitting on a park bench with Max, he was looking at her like he was planning something. Sky never read Max, it was not necessary, she knew him too well.

Finally, he looked into her eyes and said, squeezing her hand in his: "I love you, Sky..."

The difference between Max and the other guys was that he didn't need her to answer, he knew it already. He just needed to say it, for himself, not asking for anything in return.

"So stupid of you..."

"Why?"

"You already know why, Max." Sky was looking away, trying to hide her sadness and not to look into his eyes.

"No, I don't..."

"Devil cannot love..."

They broke up after one month, but Max never stopped calling her 'devil'.

Remembering that day, Sky was wondering if it would be the same with Ben. He called her 'little devil' and how ironic that sounded?! Ben was different. Her feelings were also not like before, but Sky was wondering if she was capable of falling in love... or, once again, she would need to charge her feelings from the guy just to keep relationships alive, like she did with Max.

He was different from others, and it was inspiring. She wanted to make it right this time. And he talked about exclusivity already. Sky grimaced... Nothing ever stopped her from doing what she wanted. She didn't want to feel trapped or changed by him. He sounded serious enough, maybe he was even ready to tell her parents about them. Oh, how much fun would she have, watching their reactions and his worries!

• • • •

"I need to tell you something."

Ben didn't expect to hear Sue's voice, he didn't even feel Sky pulling her phone out of the pocket and typing. Probably he was falling asleep. It was late, Sky was quiet, and this ridiculously comfortable couch was always making him sleepy.

"Sure." He said, rubbing his eyes. "Anyway, this movie is no fun."

"Try to watch it with someone who'll be able to discuss it with you."

This was the first time Sky said something like this. Not being able to talk literally never bothered her, at least it always seemed this way. It could be less convenient for people around her, but not for Sky. Ben turned in her direction so fast that she almost fell, losing the point of support.

"What's wrong?" Ben was not feeling sleepy anymore. He was looking straight into silver eyes, not recognizing their expression. It was harsh and cold, even cruel. Something was out.

"I'm leaving..." Sky was still typing, but a thousand thoughts appeared in Ben's mind.

"Home?" He was not able to sit quietly, so suggested the most obvious possibility. She changed her mind, she doesn't want to spend this night with him, watching this stupid movie. Damn, it was boring! Of course, she'd rather go home. She was bored with him....

Ben was not able to totally convince himself. Sue started to talk again.

"I'm having sort of a book tour. Max and I are going around the country, introducing the book, signing... and other things, I'm not even sure what those things are. But it is not important. I will be gone for a month, maybe two..."

Ben froze "Book tour... Max ... gone for a month..." These were the only words his brain considered important, ripping them out of conversation and repeating all over.

Sky was obviously waiting for him to say something. Ben squeezed out a small fake smile, breathing out words one by one: "Book?"

"Oh, yes. I wrote a book. Max gave it to someone in his publishing office. They probably liked it, so they offered me this promotional tour. He is going with me because... he's my friend... and I'm not the kind of talker you can imagine introducing a book in front of a bunch of people..."

"Max?" This was Ben's way to ask if he knows who the hell was this guy.

"I'm not sure if you met him. We've been friends for years. It's the guy I met last week. Remember I told you?"

"Your ex-boyfriend?"

Sky nodded and smiled, appreciating that Ben remembered. He was trying to sound cool, but it didn't work so well. On the opposite side of the couch, Sky was completely calm and confident, smiling. She looked like she was telling him about an exciting book she found.

"When...?"

"Next week." Sky had it already typed on the keyboard, so she answered too quickly, like she just wanted to finish with all these questions already.

"No... When the hell were you planning to tell me about it?" Ben looked angry now. He was angry, confused, and jealous. Anything but happy and supportive as she expected him to be.

Sky saw it and for a second, she backed off, looking like a cat standing on her tiptoes, not knowing what to expect from a sudden enemy. Her beautiful gray eyes became cold and cruel again.

"Now."

"How long have you known?"

Sky looked annoyed and defensive now: "Since I received this offer... Maybe a couple of weeks... or a month."

"Oh, I see."

Sky didn't type, looking like she didn't understand him, like he was speaking in a foreign language.

"I just don't get it Sky! Next week? Didn't you think I should know?"

"You should definitely work on your supportive tone, mister!"

"Supportive!?" Ben was almost shouting.

Sky didn't calm down either. She was attacking: "Who are you to know this before everyone else?"

"Your…" Ben stopped for a second, realizing that he cannot pronounce what he was planning to, because Sue was ahead of him.

"UNCLE?"

"How very nice of you to play this card now, Sky, not before making love to me for the first time on this couch!"

"Should I? You sound like you're regretting…"

"Don't you put it on me, little devil! I don't regret anything! If I had a chance to change our past, I would never do that, because I never felt so happy in my life." Ben was almost shouting the last phrase, not having time to stop and realize what exactly he was saying. "Thank you so much for making me fall in love with you and leaving. What is this? My payback from the universe?"

Only after a few seconds Ben finally realized that he was walking around the couch, shouting and not even looking in her direction. He shook his head, calming down, realizing, seeing that the alerted cat turned into a kitten, that her eyes were soft and peaceful again. She was sitting on her knees, holding her phone, tapping with her nails on its metal frame, searching for the right words.

"I'm sorry. I should not say that. You're right, I am the uncle here, I should behave as an adult."

"Try to shout at me again like this and you will never see me again."

"You're losing the point, woman. I just said that I'm in love with you and you can only focus on my tone?"

"No, you're losing the point, Ben. I heard that and I accepted it. I'm sorry that you feel this way... so stupid of you." Sky had a déjà vu. It was exactly what she told Max before...

"I guess..."

"I think I should go home."

"No. Don't. Stay. What is wrong with you? Running away already? Didn't you ever have a fight with your boyfriends before?" Ben looked at Sky with an evil smile. He was completely calm now, looking like he knew something she didn't.

Sky was stunned. This look in his eyes intrigued her. Ben was not as typical as she thought he was. He was strong enough to be her opponent, he was smart enough to understand how to deal with her.

Devilish look in Ben's eyes was even more obvious now: "Was I right about a fight?" He knew he was, he just needed to hear it from her.

Sky smiled back to him: "You know you were..." How did he know, was the other question.

"So, why aren't you running away now?" He whispered.

"Because you just gave me a reason to stay."

In one short second Ben liquidated all the distance between them, squeezing her in his arms, kissing with such a passion he thought he was not capable of before, ripping his own t-shirt from her tiny body. He was turned on like never before because of this new feeling... he was one step closer to this girl, one step up to reaching Sky.

. . . .

"You're not stepping out of this house until you need to actually start your book tour." Ben was holding a tray with a freshly cooked breakfast, looking at Sky hiding under her pillow. She was trying to avoid noise he made on purpose. But he meant to wake her up.

"You didn't even cook this by yourself! Nice life having a butler, huh?"

"I have pancakes with cherry jam and chocolate here..."

Sky demonstrated interest by showing her face from under a pillow: "Now we're talking!"

"I mean it, Babe. Stay with me these days..."

"Don't you need to show up to work?"

"I'll sort it out..." Ben didn't think about it. He was not sure that he could skip work, but he couldn't be defeated by her so soon.

"Doesn't Vic's girlfriend check in like... tomorrow?"

Ben bit the corner of his bottom lip. He completely forgot about Val.

"She is not his girlfriend."

"Yeah, right." Sky couldn't hold this reaction. Too late to realize that she was not willing to discuss it. She rushed to change the subject: "Even if you don't mind her seeing me imprisoned in your house, there is one more tiny detail. You will be the one explaining to your sister why her daughter suddenly started to spend so much time with her uncle."

"We should tell Ace..."

Sky didn't expect that card to be beaten: "No, we shouldn't!"

"Tell me one reason why not?"

"She is going through a lot of pressure at work..."

"Not convincing."

"We haven't decided if it's serious between us..."

"Are you joking??? I brought you breakfast in bed!"

"You didn't cook it!"

"I'm ready to get fired from my work for taking a bunch of unreasonable days off!"

"Not convincing."

"You're crazy! Can't you see what you are doing to me?"

"Probably making you irresponsible..."

"We should tell her..."

"When we both agree on that!"

"Why are you against it? What are you expecting to happen while you're away?"

"You can do whatever you want with whoever you want while I'm away. It will not change anything."

"Huh..." Ben was shocked. With no doubts karma hit him hard. He was receiving the same attitude from Sky, the same one he had before with women. She didn't show any sign of jealousy. He shook away this feeling, changing the subject of this conversation: "So, now when I'm allowed to do whatever I want..."

"If you want to tell Ace, it's fair. But let me think about it first."

"Same way you're still thinking about our exclusivity?"

"I've got a lot on my mind..."

"Did anyone ever tell you how different you are?"

Sky couldn't hold a laugh: "Every single person I meet!"

It was not about Sky not talking, or her abilities. Ben meant her attitude. He was amazed with how this girl made him feel. One moment she was as close as his soulmate, sharing and sensitive. Another second, she was becoming unknown and undiscovered, wild and unreachable. If Ben could describe her, he would compare her to a book, written by two totally different people, who were not communicating with each other at all regarding the subject of their creation.

• • • •

"Sky!? Really!? Thank God I still have a daughter. I started to have doubts already." Sky caught me by surprise. I was sitting in the kitchen, looking at the oven, trying to convince myself that ordering food delivery for one person is pathetic, and I should rather cook. "I'm happy you're here, I almost convinced myself to cook."

"How bored are you?"

"I think spending so much time in the restaurants made me believe that cooking is not that difficult."

"This new job is affecting your brain, mother. Cooking – BAD, delivery – GOOD!"

We both started laughing and I realized that I missed laughing like this with her, being alone with her... People say that kids grow fast and mine is not making it easier by traveling first and with those disappearances lately... She didn't tell me where she was going or what she was doing there. I didn't ask. Not like I was not interested, I just know her well. I am already her most trusted person, there is no point pushing her to tell me everything. It probably would not even work with common children, not to mention this one. No one could ever make Sky do something she didn't want. She always knew what was better for her, and I must admit that she was always right.

Sometimes it felt like she had her story written already and she was blindly following it, stubbornly rejecting all the advices. I suspected a couple of dozen times that she could see the future, but I never had any evidence... She never caught a glass, falling from a table, feeling it before it happened. Nothing like that stuff in the movies either. We never won lotteries... Maybe I'm just imagining it, but I think it works the same way as reading thoughts, but in this case apparently rules are stricter. Thinking about it I remembered her confused look when for the first time she had a nosebleed caused by erasing my memories. Rules... I've been thinking a lot about this lately. Maybe I was meant to raise her, to be the kind of parent she needed, to understand and support her. I'm wondering if she even needed to be raised, it felt like she did it by herself and I was just standing next to her, just in case if she needed me.

"Ask already..." Sky decided that my silence was connected somehow to her secret staycations.

"Should I?"

"Don't you want to know?"

"I respect your privacy, my child."

"But..."

"I know you'll tell me when the time is right." I certainly didn't want to go against the universe plan. Sky bit her lip. It felt like deep inside she wanted to tell me more than I wanted to ask.

After a short pause, she typed: "Maybe we can use this time for some of this 'mother-daughter stuff'..."

I looked back at the oven, happy that now I had a proper excuse not to cook today.

"What do you have in mind?"

"...And the worst part is... You know, she is so supportive and understanding..."

"Oh, poor Max! Your girlfriend is supportive. What a bitch!"

"Shush, lady! You know exactly what I mean. She reacted differently from what I expected..."

"Speaking of unexpected reactions. Ben almost ripped my head off when I told him."

Max put the spoon with pistachio ice cream in his mouth, leaving it there for a while, meanwhile looking suspicious and thoughtful.

"I can understand that. It's normal to be jealous, especially to me." He pushed his glasses up his nose. He thought this signature move made him look smarter and sexier at the same time.

"I told him that he is free to do whatever he wants when I leave."

"What?" Max jumped on the couch, so his glasses slid down to the tip of his nose again. "You're not making it easy for him, Babe."

"It just felt right..."

"Something is wrong with your sense of direction. Do you even want to continue these relationships?"

"And... they are not official yet..."

Max burst into laughing: "This guy must be really special if you're testing him like this. And he is a saint if he'll survive all your tortures. If I was never there, I would advise him to run away from you as fast as he can..."

"He is... different..."

"Is this your way of saying that you're finally in love?"

"It is my way of saying that he is blurring my way. When I'm with him, I'm confused. I always know what should be done, but Ben... he..."

"Makes it unclear?"

Sky nodded. He had no idea.

She whispered: "I had a dream today. I was standing, facing the direction sign in the middle of nowhere. But there was nothing written on it, only empty space on wooden arrows. I was holding a marker in my hand like I meant to write it by myself. I couldn't do it because I didn't know what to write. I heard Ben's voice, he just said softly that I need just to listen to my heart. I smiled and touched my chest, trying to feel the heartbeat, but.... I couldn't, there was no heartbeat... like I was empty inside. And then it became dark, and I heard this really creepy voice whispering... The devil cannot love. I freaked out and woke up."

"Did you watch a horror movie again?"

"Really?"

Max's face became more serious.

"So maybe you just need to stop limiting yourself?"

"You sound like a self-help book now."

"Isn't that what you told me?" Sky noticed a sad note in his voice, like it was still hurting him. "Devil cannot love.... Is that what you're thinking about yourself? Do you think you're so different that you're not capable of emotions? You consider yourself shallow. Why are you punishing yourself? Or what are you punishing yourself for?"

Sky was stunned. It was not typical for Max to be that serious. She underestimated him, believing that he saw only what she was showing him. But was he right? Since the incident with Vic, she couldn't feel anything even similar to love. She thought she couldn't, but Ben popped up in her life and it was different because now she actually wanted to feel, but it still didn't happen. He seemed to be the right guy, all this looked like something that meant to be, but she still didn't feel it... Maybe Max was right, and she just limited herself? Sky felt broken. That's why she was happy for the opportunity to run away.

"One day I will not even recognize you."

"Like when I consider a plastic surgery?"

"Over my dead body. Can't you see how beautiful you are? Why do you need to change anything?"

Kim looked at her reflection on a dark TV screen and smiled, "Thanks to good genes."

I smiled. My teenage daughter looked like a typical rock fan. Leather jacket, ripped jeans, ring in her nose, heavy make-up and now... pink hair. How happy I was that it was only one night look and after that she will look less dangerous again... but with still pink hair, I guess.

Kim was putting her massive earphones on, when I waved, gesturing that I didn't finish talking. She looked at me again.

"You know the rules..." I was behaving as a responsible father now.

Kim smiled, "There are no rules."

"There are. Don't get in trouble..."

"It's not a rule. It's a common sense. Don't worry, dad. I'll be alright."

I knew she would be. Kim didn't need my supervision, not now, not in the past. I had an incredibly special child, but it didn't take any special effort to raise her by myself. My wife ran away from us when Kim was only a few months old. She never made it through massive depression after the child was born. It felt like she was completely drained after delivery, like she didn't have any power, any emotions, any life in her.

For those few months I was living in a house with an extremely radiant and cheerful newborn baby, who failed all the newborn stereotypes... and a wife that looked like an emotionless ghost. When Kim's mother disappeared, I found a note saying "I'm sorry, Pete, it's too hard for me. I will return when I feel better, to be with two of you." It was seventeen years ago. Not like I'm still waiting...

After a couple of months of single fatherhood, I realized one more thing that changed my life. My daughter could not hear. That was one of the reasons for her being the calmest baby I ever saw. She never bothered to cry as she didn't see the point of it. Why did she need to make sounds if she was not able to hear them by herself?

So, now this angel is all grown up and still gives no troubles and zero attitude, to me at least. Should I be worried about her going to this concert? Should I be worried about her at all? She always knew how to live her life better than I did. She was never a child in a family. That's why I feel so lost in these kinds of moments, not knowing what to say or what the rules are. And she was right, there were no rules. I always thought that I would be a father, coming back home after a tough day at work, fetching a child running to me and kissing my wife on her forehead. What do I have instead? I have something better...

The starting point was the day I quit my job and decided to take care of my child by myself. I was not an office father, coming home from work anymore. That day I was just sitting and staring at Kim, who was curling on a carpet in the middle of the room, playing with her favorite toys. If you can call it so. She was so focused that I couldn't even think of disturbing her. My barely year-old Kim was busy punching with a spoon everything she could find. She somehow realized that all these things should sound different. What do you hear punching the sofa or the wooden table with a spoon? Nothing significant, I guess. Maybe you'll even choose to ignore it, because who on earth needs this sound? My daughter chose to need it. She was patiently exploring all the possible vibrations, creating more and more of them. The moment I noticed that, I went to a shop and bought the best stereo system I could find, so my angel could listen to music. Shortly after that I received a few complaints from neighbors, but nothing I couldn't sort out with a wide smile and sincere apology.

I was mostly the only father on the kids' playgrounds. All the mothers admired me for my unique and non-traditional way of raising a child. I just didn't care about rules and standards, I was just being there for Kim with a huge bag of toys and earphones... just in case she needed me. But that child... you could never guess what she needed. One second you find her throwing the stones in the fountain, in a split moment she was already sitting on the knees of a complete stranger and looking into his eyes.

"Oh, that look... It feels like she stares straight into your soul." *Said one of the mothers on the playground once about Kim.*

No one could resist her, just one look at this cutie with blond locks and black eyes and you forgot about the rest of things. And the little one was addicted to people, it felt like she was aiming to explore as much company as she could, moving constantly from one unfamiliar person to another.

"How lucky you are! My son is so shy, he barely communicates with other kids, not talking about adults." *Said the other mommy ones.*

I bet she would not consider me lucky after seeing me pulling Kim from a homeless guy on the bench, cleaners removing garbage bins, subway musicians. She wanted to communicate with every single person on her way and I... learned to carry sanitizer with me all the time.

"How are you doing that? You have such a level of understanding with her." Said the other playground mother one day.

Signing language was not an option in our case. I tried multiple ways to communicate with Kim, we attended one lesson of signing language together, well... we attended 10 minutes of it. When Kim realized where we were and what we were trying to learn, she looked at me in a way I will never forget. She was disappointed. I never tried to do that again.

I could not explain how we communicated with Kim or when she learned to read my lips. The only thing I knew was that my daughter wanted to be different, not limited.

When she was 3, other people appeared to be less happy with my unique parenting techniques, saying that I am not doing good enough for the father of a special child. Apparently, according to standards, children should talk or sign, in our case, by this age. Mommies became worried. I tried to ignore it, but the fear was crawling deep inside of me. What if I did something wrong? After one more conversation about it, I was standing in my kitchen, opening a bottle of beer, beating myself up for being a terrible father. Kim was sitting in front of the TV watching the news when I first heard her.

"Music..."

My 3-year-old was sitting on the couch, holding a remote control in her tiny hands, struggling with pressing a tight button to change a channel... to music channel, I guess. The beer bottle almost slipped from my hand to the floor. It was the first time my daughter talked.

She didn't sound like anything I heard before. She didn't sound like I expected her to sound. After one short second I was on my knees next to Kim, begging her to repeat what I had just heard. She looked at me like she knew something I didn't or couldn't. She dropped the remote on the floor and touched my face with her palm.

"Upset..."

Now I knew that I was not dreaming, and she actually did it before. Kim sounded so different... She sounded like an internal voice, clear but distant at the same time.

"No, not upset, my love. You'll never upset me." I said with tears streaming down my cheeks to her tiny hands. I always kept this promise.

Next day I was the proudest parent ever sitting on the bench and watching Kim surrounded by other kids, epically saying to playground moms that I don't care about rules and standards. I refused to ever be disappointed with my daughter and I promised to let her be as different as she wanted to be. If she wanted to be the only deaf person on earth that didn't know the signing language, let it be.

That day I was so inspired by her that I pulled out of the dark and dusty corner of my wardrobe the box I hadn't opened for years. It was full of memories and photos, but that was not what I was looking for. I pulled out all the notebooks I ever started writing in, all the stories I never finished, all ideas I had but never started implementing them. It was time to write now. If my daughter could be the person she wanted, what was stopping me from doing the same?

Now I can tell that I would never be able to do that without Kim, that's why I dedicate to her every book I write. But this time I was not only writing, I was also brave enough to publish.

After all those years I can say that I became quite successful in what I do, not only writing by myself, but also helping unknown authors to reach their dreams. With a lot of help from my friend Jen I opened a publishing agency and became a big boss. One of things I did right about my business, was not overdoing it. I never sacrificed my life and Kim for it. I worked exactly as much and as productively as I wanted and built a massive company of people committed to their jobs as much as I did, of people loving their jobs.

· · · ·

"Pete... Are you even listening to me?"

"I will start listening when your words become more interesting than my salad. Please don't waste my precious lunch break."

Max was sitting opposite of me in the diner. He looked like a teenager, asking his parents to give him a car for the first time.

"I want you to meet her..." Max was mumbling.

I realized that I skipped the beginning of the conversation. My brain searched for an answer. What can Max be so shy about? Huh... The girl. The one he's talking nonstop about.

"I didn't read the manuscript..."

"I know, you gave it to Jen."

"Did she read it?"

"She said it's brilliant."

"So, what do you want from me? Jen can deal with it."

"I want you to meet her."

"Max, I know I look like a lonely and miserable man, but I'm not looking for a girlfriend."

Apparently, the joke was not understood as Max's face became red and he pushed his glasses all the way up his nose.

"I'm not here to supply 19-year-old girlfriends for you! I just want you to meet her."

"Tell me one reason I should do it, not Jen."

"She will be your bestselling author."

"Idea with a girlfriend was more attractive, man!"

"Ok, she is different..."

"Like any single person on this planet. And my salad is becoming more interesting now..."

"Since when you're eating salads?"

"Since my daughter started assessing her new food theory. I'm supporting her in this... and everything else, I guess."

Max became even more stressed and shy at the same time. I couldn't torture him any longer. He is a good guy, but he needs more experience if he wants to be successful in the publishing business.

"I want you to convince her to publish..." Saying that Max exhaled, like something huge just fell of his chest.

"So, you want to tell me that she doesn't want to publish, and I need to convince her. Isn't that what you should do? You're her friend, right?"

"Yeah, like she ever listens to me."

"I like her already. I think we have something in common."

"You should do it, dad!" Max jumped in his chair as he didn't notice a tall person in oversized sports clothes behind him, until she started talking.

"You don't even know what it is about, Honey."

"Who cares? He is asking for something. You can see it in the way he's sitting like a schoolboy in a director's office."

"Join us, you psychic."

Kim dropped her sports bag on the floor next to the vacant chair and sat on it. I looked at her with the overwhelming feelings of a proud father. Undoubtedly oversized sports clothes, zero makeup, short pink hair tight in a tail. She looked like a total mess. No high hills or tight short shorts, no heavy makeup with fake eyelashes that can reach her forehead. She was extremely natural and totally refused fashion cannons. All the other girls of her age looked exactly opposite. But how jealous they were of her. Guys just couldn't resist Kim. I guess, nothing changed since her childhood. She could just come to the guy, look at him with these huge deep black eyes, and he was stunned.

Her girlfriends asked her how she did it. Kim always laughed, saying "I just look straight into their souls."

"Max, meet my daughter Kim."

"I didn't know you would be here... did I ruin your plans?"

Kim looked at his mouth, biting her bottom lip "I cannot hear you, silly. At least not what you're saying."

Max was obviously shocked, as he didn't understand if she was serious. She sounded so clear, but distant.

"It takes practice. I will need to talk to you few more times to learn to read your lips."

"You can't hear me... I know a bit of sign language. My cousin is deaf, so I learned it when we were children."

"You can sign if you want, I will not understand it. I don't know sign language. You people are so funny with your standard decisions." Kim laughed softly. "Sorry gentleman, I need to use the ladies room."

Max couldn't stop staring at her while she was walking away from the table. He looked at me with a total confusion.

"She is..."

"Deaf, yeah, I know." I have been through this conversation so many times that I could predict almost every reaction already."

"No, I mean, yes... But she is amazing."

"Oh, right. But don't expect a promotion or something if you date her."

"I... What the hell are you talking about?"

"Just joking, man. Relax."

At this moment, the waiter arrived at the table, putting a glass with something green in it on the table. It looked like blended grass.

"Mr. Pete, can you please tell her it's from me? I hope she likes it."

"Oh, let's see... It looks undoubtedly healthy and extremely non-edible and undrinkable. Sure, Ted, she'll love it! Why won't you say it yourself?"

"Maybe another time, sir."

Poor guy... Maybe after a few more years of us coming here, he would finally be able to ask Kim out. I continued my thoughts aloud, seeing Max's confusion.

"It has been happening for a while already... The first time they met he was so shy and confused, especially when he realized that Kim is special. Now, he never serves our table anymore and tries to grab her attention with those gifts..."

"Does it work?"

"I don't think so. Kim is very personal. When she doesn't communicate with people in real life, she sort of loses a connection."

"Not a social media person, huh?"

"You got it right."

Max became quiet and excused himself shortly after Kim came back. I noticed that he had something on his mind now, something about my daughter. But it was not the common interest, it was something bigger this time. I got curious and made a mental note to myself to find out what was happening in his mind that day.

• • • •

There was a weird conversation that happened when Kim was 12. It still feels unfinished to me, like I didn't ask enough questions then. This was the kind of conversation that keeps you thinking about it from time to time, not letting you go.

Kim was in the kitchen behind the bar, making a special evening drink for me. At least 2 out of ten drinks she made were totally drinkable. Don't you dare to judge me for supporting my 12-year-old in her bartending hobby! She had a lot of fun, and I had a variety of interesting drinks on my cocktail menu.

"If you had a choice to be normal, able to blend in with the general crowd on the planet, or to be special... different from everyone else... what would you choose." She suddenly asked.

For a moment, I felt myself in the motivational seminar about self-improvement and empowerment.

"Do you mean something different, my angel? It feels like it is not a question you really want to ask. What's bothering you?"

Kim shook her head, pressing her palms on the bar stand, like she was trying to leave her handprints in the cement.

"What do you think, if people could actually choose it... will there be more special ones around?"

"There are a lot of special people on this planet, Honey."

Kim shook her head again. What I was saying didn't match with what she wanted to hear.

"That's not what I mean, dad. I just can't understand it. It's so stupid of them. This world is so dumb..."

I was thinking that my little one was becoming a teenager with raging internal conflict, but I was wrong. Kim never showed any further signs of a regular emotional teen, no drama, no more annoyance with all those people that chose to be normal. There was only one change I've noticed in her behavior. She stopped being so tactile as she was before, trying to touch every single person whether she knew them or not. Since that day I have never seen my daughter shaking hands with another person or touching the bare skin of someone else. She was constantly apologizing, saying that she has an allergy to something on other people's skin, but I never believed in that. None of her medical tests showed that and I never saw any sign of rash on her hands. I was sure that the reason was made out, because Kim never stopped touching me or someone in an emergency situation.

When I was completely sure that my daughter was hiding something, we talked again.

"What's up with the allergy story, Hon?"

"I just don't feel like touching other people, dad..."

"You cannot cut yourself out like this. One day you'll have a boyfriend and avoiding holding hands will kill part of the romance."

She looked at me like I scared her with something, but that look disappeared in a moment.

"So, I will not have a boyfriend. I'll spend all my life with you, because you're the only man I love to touch!"

Kim laughed and hugged me, proving her theory in practice. It was flattering to hear from her, but I was still wondering if I asked enough questions that day.

Ben was sitting and drinking alone, going through all the things he had been regretting since Sky left. How hard could it be just to wait for her without any accidents?

First, was Val... second, all the other girls from his past and present, who attacked... When you're desperate to find a couple (not like he ever was!), no one wants you, but when you finally find someone and relax, you're getting a queue of candidates wanting to be with you. It's like they feel that something shifted inside of you, that you're happy and satisfied now, so they want to be happy together with you.

The difference was, Ben never experienced lack of ladies in his life, but now they wanted relationships. Like someone announced on the radio "Dear Ladies, Ben is finally ready to have serious relationships and fall in love. If you're interested, please call or meet him for further details. Good luck. Let the best win!"

Val recognized him from the moment he opened the door of his house to welcome her.

'Cutie in black.' Just popped up in her mind, even though Ben was wearing a blue t-shirt this time. From the moment she stepped into his house, horny Val was activated, and she knew exactly what she was doing.

How many times did Ben see her near the pool in a bikini that was barely covering anything? Once, she knocked on his room door wearing only a towel, saying that there was no hot water in her shower. She didn't expect that he would politely send her to try her luck in the other guest room. The other time she was almost offering herself to him when they were watching a movie together.

Ben remembered the night and continued squeezing his glass in hand. That was intense. Even watching Val daily was quite challenging. She had this kind of dangerous aura, pulling you in like a vortex. Ben wanted to be pulled in and forget everything. The devil on his shoulder was hungry, advising him to take a chance, convincing him that Sky would never find out about it. Angel was not that talkative, just reminding him that if he wanted Val so much, maybe Sky was not so special to him.

That night Ben was planning to stop drinking until Val finally moved out, because alcohol made him lose focus on what he really wanted. He was sitting on the couch, watching the movie. Val was on the other side of the couch. He tried to remember how they ended up doing it together, but couldn't. He was charmed by Val. So simple and open, not even a bit ashamed of her desires. On her second day in his house, she told him, looking straight into his eyes, that they met once in the bar and since that day she wanted him. He explained to her that he had a girlfriend... sort of.

"Sort of?" Val knew exactly what questions to ask.

"It's complicated..."

"Should it be? If it's not that clear and not official, maybe it's not even exclusive?"

Ben's heart started to ache because she was saying exactly what he didn't want to hear.

"It is something special."

"How do you know that it's special if you're not even sure that it's real?"

"It is real!"

"So where is she? Why isn't she pulling my hair out for flirting here with you? Does she even know that I'm here?"

Ben didn't want to have this conversation anymore. it was hurting him. She was sitting here, so simple and open, on the couch that held memories of Sky. Then Val touched his hand, looking at him like a trusted friend. That was the moment when he knew everything. Her touch was like the touch of any other lady in his life. He didn't feel it. She was not Sky and that was enough. He took her hand in his, looked her in the eyes and said:

"Not going to happen."

"What?" Val looked surprised.

"Nothing going to happen between us. You can walk naked around me, touch my hand and stare with this romantic look. You can do whatever you feel like. I may want you, but I need someone else, and you are not her. You cannot be."

For the first time in his love life, Ben didn't choose the easy, he wanted something complicated now.

· · · ·

"Angels..." Ter sounded extremely excited, not even trying to hide the fact that he was enjoying his own joke.

"Bosley..." Kim sounded so arrogant that Ter realized that the joke he planned for days was crushed in a few seconds.

"Mood killer..."

"Babe, I don't even need to hear your jokes to crush them."

"You're evil." Ter looked surprised and suspicious at the same time.

"Should we at least sit?" Sky was getting annoyed with people staring at Ter and Kim, expecting some sort of drama from them. "Maybe we can at least try to get discreet? Isn't that the main point of this thing?"

"Secret society meeting... There is something special... Should it not be public?" Kim was not hiding her irony looking around the busy diner which had only one table empty, reserved for them.

"Sit" Sky said it with the widest and the brightest fake smile she was capable of. She pointed at the empty table.

"Grumpy?" Ter was mouthing the word to Kim, making sure that Sky saw it as well.

Kim nodded, putting her earphones in the bag, saying: "Missing a boyfriend, I guess".

They both felt how Sky's muscles tensed and giggled.

When they approached the table, Ter nodded, giving way to Kim with a small curtsy: "After you, Kimberly".

Kim nodded theatrically: "Terrance".

"Oh, very gentle this time," Ter said, kissing her hand, which he received to assist a lady with the sitting.

"I practiced." Kim was barely holding from bursting into laughter.

It was their small ritual. Calling full names, pretending to be a lady and the gentleman of god knows which century, attracting as much attention from people around them. Sky hated it, but it was becoming better after that, so she was just casually browsing her phone to let them finish. She couldn't help but notice that Kim did look more like a lady today, wearing a wide and long dirty greenish color dress which looked like it could fit three of her. She still didn't cheat her nature though and was wearing sneakers. Sky couldn't recall the time she saw Kim wearing a skirt before. For the moment she even thought about how cool Kim would look, wearing something even more girly. She had the body of a supermodel, but with very cool and natural curves. Most ladies would kill for the body like hers, but this one was just wasting it under all these bulky clothes.

"Are you working out?" Kim was admiring Ter's biceps now.

He did look different also. Sky looked at Ter again hearing this, still browsing through social media on her phone with her finger. Last time they met, Ter looked messier. If she didn't know him, Sky would assume that he was sleeping on the park bench. But today she could see the changes. His ginger hair and beard were recently trimmed and shaved, he looked fitter and even a bit taller. Even his clothes looked like they were ironed. He was the same height as Ben... Thinking about it, Sky banged her forehead to the wooden table, trying to remove Ben out of her head. It's been more than a month since book tour started, and she saw him.

"Ter..." Sky whispered, not taking her face from the table surface. "Please start talking". Her voice was not angry or frustrated anymore, it was desperate.

Ter's face became serious at once. He looked at Kim with a silent question in his eyes: "That bad?" Kim made a barely visible movement with her shoulders. She didn't know.

"Let's order first. We don't want to be the kind of customers, who just occupy the space in the busy restaurant." Ter's voice was more reassuring now, there was no more space for jokes. Time was not right, and he knew it.

After drinks were served, Ter started talking very officially, like at a particularly important board meeting. When they met, his eyes looked playful and goldish in color, now serious and deep brown.

"Today we're here to discuss, how Sky is busy ruining 'the plan' and the life of her uncle."

"Damn it, Ter..." Sky was talking through her teeth, her eyes also became darker with a devilish twinkle in it. "You're not in position to judge..."

"Am I?" Ter interrupted her, with the same dominating twinkle in his eyes. Nice and smiley guy was gone for the second.

"Should we all relax for a second?" Kim felt a need to break the tension. They both looked at her like she was the enemy, but she was not. "We all know that 'the plan' is not reliable."

Ter made a 'whatever' gesture. Sky sighed.

Sky started talking with the tone of a schoolteacher, explaining to small kids why it is not allowed to run in the school corridor: "When I asked you what to do, you sent me on this stupid book trip".

"Stupid? Really? At least that was according to 'the plan'!" Ter folded his hands, showing how hurt he was.

"Don't be a baby, Ter! My life is getting complicated here." After seeing that Ter didn't react, Sky added peacefully: "I'm sorry for calling book tour stupid. I know it was important, I just..." She didn't know what to say next, just squeezed her phone in her hands, hoping that Sue would pick it up from there.

"You can do anything you want..." Ter sounded peaceful now.

"It's the first time I hear something like this from you." Sky was obviously shocked.

For the first time in years, Ter was not going to teach her how to live her life, how to avoid trouble, how to follow 'the plan'. It was always so frustrating, they argued constantly... and now he was not an enemy anymore. Did he just give up on her?

This silence was annoying, even for Kim. She elbowed Ter impatiently: "Keep talking, Ter..."

"I don't have anything else for Sky..." Ter looked upset now.

"And by saying that, you mean..." Sky was not getting the hell what was going on.

"By saying that, I mean that I have no further quests for you..."

"Which means..." Sky was more impatient now.

"Which can mean one of two things: or you messed up so badly that 'the plan' is not possible to recover, or you're almost done... I can only guess now, Ok? I don't have any information! Maybe it is your time to figure it out, not mine. Maybe it is the same case when Kim refused touching people ..."

"Hey! I didn't refuse touching people!" Kim seemed offended.

"It's not about you, Babe!" Ter put his palm on hers.

"Like you would want to do it in my place..." Kim wrapped her hands around herself.

"Like getting your corrections is pure flowers and butterflies! But I'm not able to stop it and I want to help you!"

Sky was not listening to them anymore. She could think of only one thing. There was no plan anymore. It could be incredibly good, or extremely wrong. She looked at Ter again and softly said "No judgment?"

"No judgment... for now at least." He smiled with the corner of his mouth, looking even more mysterious now.

"So, all this drama today regarding me messing up Ben's life was…"

"Just my own thoughts, pure me… no one else. But it is sick, girl!"

"No one is asking for your opinion!" Sky laughed and through the tissue she was rubbing in her hands, straight in his disgusted face.

Kim was quiet, more than ever. She was just trying to absorb the facts.

"Terrance…" Sky looked straight into his goldish eyes.

"Skyler…" Ter picked up the same tone.

"If you could do anything without consequences, what would you do?"

"I would be a famous actor, rich, with a crowd of fans." Ter's eyes were glowing now. He was admiring the vision that appeared in his mind. "What about you?"

"How nice of you to ask…" Sky smiled with something Max called a 'devil smile', quickly took her bag from the chair and left the restaurant gracious and fast at the same time.

"She will go to him." Kim was still staring at the way Sky left, like she left a trace after her.

"She will…" Ter nodded.

"So why didn't you tell her the truth?" She enjoyed his surprised look and continued talking "I touched you, remember?"

"Now you know…"

"Gift and a Curse."

"You know I couldn't."

"You don't need to explain." Saying this Kim petted his messy hair, while he put his head on her shoulder.

"I need a drink."

"Do you want to go to my place? Father exceeded his collection of alcohol again." Kim giggled.

"I missed you, Kimberly... And thank you for, you know..."

"You don't need to explain." She repeated, touching his blushing cheek this time.

• • • •

Sky didn't have a chance to breathe in, to think what she should do or say. He opened the door before she managed to press the doorbell. He was going out, his jacket in his hand. He looked at her without seeing. He stopped and time stopped together with him.

"Sky..." He felt quiet and distant, like he was talking from inside the deep cave.

"Ben..." she tried to smile, but she couldn't do it. She couldn't fake it, not now, not in front of him.

She took a small step in his direction. Like a cat hunting a bird on the street, steady and patient. Ben didn't move. Sky looked him straight in the eyes. She took one more step, now being so close to him that she could hear his heart beating. Ben didn't move still. She put her hand on his chest, feeling that despite her full confidence, her fingers were shaking. He put his hand on hers, whispering: "Still there, still beating."

Sky finally smiled: "Good. I was worried."

"Little devil..."

Hearing these words, Sky also stopped feeling the ground under her feet. Ben fetched her with one hand and squeezed her into his chest so hard that it was painful for a moment. This was the best pain Sky ever experienced in her life.

• • • •

"You need to go."

"I don't care." He didn't go anywhere that day, that night. When morning approached, Sky started to be seriously worried that he might squeeze life out of her. Most of the time since her arrival, Ben was hugging her, or held her hand, even while he was sleeping, which was not typical for him at all.

"I need to go. Ace is waiting."

"I don't care. You belong to me now." Ben pronounced it with a creepy and funny voice. Sky giggled.

"Personal space, Benjamin!"

"No."

"I don't have time, Babe. I need to step by the bookstore before I go home."

Ben didn't answer.

"I shouldn't come to you first." Now Sky was laughing, trying to fight him and climb out of the bed. He was much stronger than she was, so it was physically impossible to do without him letting her do it. "I bet you never did it before." It worked, Ben's muscles relaxed, so Sky almost ended up falling on the floor by inertia.

"I didn't. It was sort of opposite. They didn't want to go." Glow of self-love and confidence shone on his face. Sky loved that look, all the ladies loved it. For a moment she imagined walking down the street holding his hand and seeing all the jealous looks... or even better, end up at the party together surrounded by his exes. She enjoyed the scene until Ter's disgusted look appeared in her memory. She shook it off as soon as she could, but Ben noticed the shift.

"What was it?"

"Nothing. Just thinking... Oh, you never told me how it went with Val."

Ben was not ready for this random attack.

"I don't want to talk about it..."

"Oh, nothing suspicious at all..."

Ben was fast forwarding in his mind all those moments when he was so absorbed by Val, almost ready to give up.

"Almost." He said quietly.

"Almost..." Sky repeated with a smile. He was sincere, Sky respected it.

"Yep, it was a tough call."

"I see.... almost is good." She said with a fake smile. Deep inside her devil was ready to squeeze life out the horny bitch. How dare Val trying to steal her Ben? "No judgment." Sky pronounced so quietly that only she could hear. Her blood was boiling. Sky never felt jealous before.

. . . .

"Sky?"

She was browsing through the bookshelves, reading all the labels, trying to find something new to read. This small bookstore was her favorite. It didn't have much to offer, but the atmosphere was adorable. She could spend hours here just diving into this warm and cozy world.

"Sky?"

This time she heard him and turned around at once, holding a book in each of her hands. His voice made her feel like her heart was echoing it.

"Vic..."

She didn't come closer, just waved to him from a few meters away. He noticed it with a surprised look in his eyes. Vic moved next to her so fast that she was not able to step aside and almost lost her balance.

"Are you Ok?" He didn't look worried, he was curious.

"Yep, all good. You?"

"Is Ben doing fine?" Vic pronounced his name louder, or Sky felt it this way. She couldn't stop herself from looking around and checking if anyone heard it. Like Vic was not casually asking about her uncle's and his colleague's wellbeing.

Vic noticed it and theatrically lowered his voice. He was teasing her. Sky was getting annoyed with him.

"We were supposed to get out together yesterday, but he just disappeared."

"I arrived yesterday." Sky was getting her confidence back now. "We were... busy."

Vic was astonished with that twinkle in her eyes. Such a shift within seconds... Vic caught himself admiring her. When she looked him in the eyes saying her last words, it felt familiar. He was looking at the most beautiful woman and he had this feeling before they met for the first time... in Ace's house, but he had no memories about it. Vic tried to shake it off, but this feeling didn't leave him for a while after.

"He was a bit lost without you..."

"Val was keeping his company, I guess."

"Val is something. It's hard to resist her." Vic smiled, thinking of how he couldn't... and secretly hoped that Ben wouldn't either.

"He is tough enough to resist, not like... others." Sky's eyes were now glowing. She barely resisted comparing tough Ben to weak Vic.

Vic felt astonished. She knew. It was not a guess. She knew that he couldn't resist Val. Familiar weird feeling was attacking him again.

After a few moments of awkward silence, they went in different directions. Sky pulled her phone to write one short message: "Damn it, Ter".

This was the moment when Vic was supposed to meet Sky.

• • • •

Is it too early for a drink?" Ter pressed a button to block his phone screen.

"Is it ever too early for anything?" Kim was standing in the middle of the kitchen, chopping lettuce next to a big salad bowl.

"Am I taking it too seriously?"

"Like this is not the most common thing you do..."

"Will you start answering my questions?" Ter hugged the couch pillow, covering his face, trying to hide from reality.

"You don't want me to." Kim was not looking at him, she was staring at her finger now, trying to figure out how badly she just sliced it with the knife, and if it was going to start bleeding.

"True..." Ter was satisfied with the answer. "If you could do anything without consequences, what would you do?" He precisely repeated the question Sky asked him earlier. It stuck in his mind, like an unresolved task.

Kim looked surprised now. She was holding her barely bleeding finger in her mouth. It didn't feel like the right time to look for a bandage.

"I'm doing it already..." She sat next to him, gently removing the pillow from his face.

"Slicing your fingers with the knife?" Ter finally noticed the red spot on her finger.

"You're an idiot."

"Interesting. That's what I'm thinking about myself lately..."

Kim smiled, touching his unshaved cheek. "Will you stop obsessing about her?"

"Jealous?" Ter was smiling now.

"Are you always saying what you think?"

"That's my job, isn't it?"

"You're so much more than the job."

"No one thinks so, but you." Ter looked her straight in the eyes, their darkness absorbed him. Kim's hand was still touching his cheek.

"That's why I exist..."

"Sounds like a very weird mission... Do you ever miss it? Having quests? Knowing what should be done?"

Kim was silent for a moment, looking at the cut on her finger.

"When I knew what should be done, I never wanted to do that. Not because my quests were difficult or weird, it just never felt like it was my choice. I hated it."

"I hate that... you don't need me anymore."

"That's the kind of relationship you want us to have? You want me to depend on you?"

"Not exactly..."

Ter was looking into the black eyes. Kim was still touching his cheek, quietly brushing his beard with her fingers.

"Maybe it is my quest..." Kim smiled sadly.

"Maybe it is our Curse?"

"Gift and a Curse..." Kim said slowly.

"If you could do anything without consequences, what would you do?" Ter was saying this phrase exactly the way Sky did it.

"I would do the only thing I'm not allowed to do."

"Dark thoughts..."

"What would you do?"

"Same..."

They both laughed. Ter hugged her and pulled her next to him so hard, it was almost painful. Kim kissed his hair, pulling away.

"So, what about a drink?"

"Aaand... she's running away." Ter went back to hugging his pillow.

· · · ·

"HOW COULD YOU DO IT?"

Ben never saw Sky so angry before. She was throwing everything she could find in his direction. Luckily, when she came in, he was in the bedroom and there were not many sharp objects. Just in case, Ben looked around, assessing the danger he was in. While he was distracted, a small neck pillow almost hit him on the head. He didn't need to ask what she was talking about. He knew. Now he just needed to survive the attack, hoping that she would calm down soon.

"How dare you make this decision without me?"

Picture frame ended up scratching Ben's arm before falling on the floor and breaking. Trying to avoid stepping into scattered glass with his bare feet, Ben lost his focus and felt a phone charger hitting his chest. Things were going out of control. His defense strategy was not working, he was forced to change it.

"Why the hell did you think that it was your decision to make?"

For a moment Sky was out of objects to throw at him, so he used this opportunity, with one fast move appearing next to her and forcing her in his hands. He didn't expect her to be so strong. With one sharp move, she pushed him away and he fell on a bed behind. He couldn't lose the moment, so he jumped up again, locking her in his arms again, this time tighter. She couldn't break out this time.

"You're a selfish coward..." Sky continued shouting into his chest, barely having enough air for it.

"I was lonely..."

"You could tell me!"

"You were unreachable on that tour..." Ben sounded so desperate; it was hurting Sky even more than her almost crushing bones.

"You could tell me today, before I went there!"

"I am a selfish coward..."

"You are!" Sky didn't expect him to agree with her.

"I told my sister that I'm in love."

"Don't you dare to put it so nicely! You told your sister that you are in love with her daughter! Without even thinking of telling me that before I went there and faced her! How could you do it?"

"She is my sister."

"And my mother!" Sky was out of breath now.

She tried to set herself free again and saw the narrow red mark on Ben's arm. It was from the frame she threw at him a few minutes ago. It scratched him badly. Seeing this she stopped fighting. Ben was still holding her tight just in case of another sudden mood swing.

"I'm sorry, Babe. She just knows me so well. And I needed to talk to someone. Sitting at home was not an option with that Val around, Vic was away... I went to Ace, and she almost knew it before I told her. I mean she knew how I felt, not the person I felt it for. She was so supportive, so I just couldn't hide it anymore."

"I'm sorry for hurting you..."

Ben didn't understand if she was talking about leaving him or scratching his arm. He noticed her looking at the mark on his hand.

"I should tell you..."

"Coward."

"Miraculously, you make me the strongest and the most vulnerable ever."

"She is happy for us... that's what she said..."

"I guess you were lucky to get this reaction." Ben finally let Sky go, rolled his trousers up and pointed at the almost invisible yellowish bruise next to his knee, saying: "This is from the candle holder from your mother's living room. You're definitely her daughter..."

Sky hid her blushing cheeks on his chest and they both laughed.

"I definitely felt the connection." Val scooped a full spoon of ice cream and held it in her mouth, enjoying the freeze reaching her brain.

"I don't remember asking you about it..." Vic didn't want to sound rude, but he was tired of listening to stories titled 'Ben and Val spending time together.'

"If I only had more time..." Val was not listening to him, still holding an empty spoon in her mouth.

Ben was now the center of her attention, not Vic. He should be happy about it, but that was not what he had on his mind now.

"It was weird. That time when we watched the movie..." Val just continued talking, she was so absorbed with her thoughts that even if Vic ran away, she wouldn't notice it.

Thinking about it, Vic looked at the café door, measuring how soon he could finally get out of this conversation. But what he saw there stopped this train of thoughts. Someone he knew was standing there. He didn't see the face, but there could not be a mistake. A tight outfit highlighted how perfectly fit she was, long silver hair was spread all over her shoulders. Vic could swear that music started playing the moment she stepped in with that gentle catwalk, that everyone around became quiet, and all eyes were on her. It was the most beautiful lady he saw in his life and the feeling of how familiar and at the same time how distant she was, was killing him.

"Sky" He didn't plan to say it out loud. It sounded weird enough that even Val stopped talking.

"Pardon?"

Vic was not listening to her anymore. When he forced himself to shift attention from Sky, shock crawled into his mind. Sky was accompanied by a guy, gently holding her by the waist. She was smiling at him, playfully putting her head on his shoulder while talking to a host about the table. He used this moment and almost visibly pulled himself closer to her and touched her silky hair with his cheek. Vic was hungrily catching every moment of it. There was only one thought piercing through his mind. Even from behind the guy looked shorter and skinnier than Vic expected. There were no doubts that it was not Ben.

He was trying not to show emotions, but Val quickly read the changes of his facial expressions. She knew him so well that she at once realized that something was happening. She turned around and looked in the same direction.

"What are you staring at?" Saying it, she immediately identified the source of his attention. Val didn't recognize the girl she saw on the bridge many years ago, but the look in Vic's eyes was so familiar. She couldn't recall seeing it before, the only thing she knew, it made her feel jealous. "Sky? Isn't it the name of Ben's..."

She stopped talking as she saw Vic's angry look.

"Shut it, Valerie."

"Apparently Ben is not the only one interested in her..." Val giggled, watching Vic staring at the couple walking to the opposite side of the café.

"Maybe he is just a friend." Vic accidentally said this aloud without actually believing in it.

Val giggled again: "I'm not talking about him, Babe."

Now Val knew something that Vic was scared to admit to himself since the moment he met Sky. He wanted to lie, he wanted her to be wrong, but managed only to say: "Damn it, Val..."

"Can I be the one to tell Ben? Please, please, please." Val happily put one more spoon of ice cream in her mouth.

Vic couldn't control himself at this moment, so for a second a scared look appeared on his face. He didn't want Ben to know about whatever feelings he had. Ben was the closest friend he had had in years, he couldn't spoil it, not like this.

"Not about you, Silly!" Val was genuinely enjoying the shifts in his facial expressions. "I mean about her cheating Ben with that new guy." After a moment of silence, Val continued thinking aloud without expecting Vic to answer. "Some ladies just can't get enough. She has everything most girls would kill for, but see... Apparently, he can't satisfy her needs... It's ok, I'll take him if she doesn't need him..."

"Shut it, Val..." Vic through the angry look across the table again.

"You remind me about my ex-husband, Victor, always trying to shut me up..."

"Nice comparison, Val... I'm just trying to think..." He sounded apologetic but didn't actually mean it.

"Will you introduce me?" Val jumped in her chair, grabbing Vic's hand with her both.

That was not the worst idea. Vic was dying to know who the guy was. He was a detective. His blood was boiling for investigation. He needed to know, not only for Ben.

• • • •

Later that day Vic was sitting at home staring at the picture on the wall. Thinking about Sky, wondering if he should go to her table and hear excuses from her, or was he right pulling Val from the café almost forcefully, not letting her interact with Sky.

Vic was looking at the picture he drew a few years ago. He remembered how he was craving to express something he didn't understand then. Dark silhouette of a man, with his hand up, looking like he was trying to reach the endless sky filled with stars.

"Suicide mission, man..." He said to a silhouette on his painting.

I would lie if I said that I remember when it started. I thought about it so many times that I don't know what the truth is anymore. I probably was born with it, same as my girls. It just took me longer to realize that I was different.

Kim has this theory that we chose to be special. Did we actually have this choice? Did my soul decide that I don't want to be like any other human, that I want to have a gift, that I want something to be taken from me in return? It's hard to judge now. I just don't remember...

I was around 5 years old when I started drawing pictures. That's what my mom told me. She was so proud that her boy had artistic potential. She was attending art classes in college but had to quit her dream to find a more reliable career. So, imagine her face when she saw her little boy scribbling something on a paper.

The only thing she didn't know was that I was not imagining, I was just transferring pictures in my head to a paper. I was not a creator... I was a messenger.

I do remember the first time I made a drawing of Sky. I guess she was not even born than... Tiny, but not a fragile, with the shiny locks of gray hair framing her face. My mother asked who the girl was. I was scribbling for hours straight. I opened my mouth to say her name, but a deep, rusty voice in my head interrupted me with "Don't..."

I remember looking around myself in confusion, not understanding what had just happened. But I listened to the voice, my instincts made me confident that it was the only way.

"I don't know." I mumbled and started to draw a tree next to Sky, to distract mother's attention.

And I just kept drawing, privately from now on, probably scared of this weird voice, not allowing me to talk about it.

I got the album and was religiously hiding it from other eyes. There was no way that Sky was not real, with all the details I saw. It felt like I was watching a silent movie about her but had no idea why or what I should do about it. Until that day.

I remember waking up with the nagging desire to go out. That was slightly ruining my plan of spending a day playing video games. It was still early, but the sense of urgency was unbearable, it was like I've been pushed by invisible force. I lazily pulled my clothes on.

"OK, OK, I'm doing it. No need to be so pushy." I was sure I heard grumpy mumbling in return.

I pushed my album in a backpack and was on my way. Sleepiness was not hiding the fact that I was excited, man on my first mission. Before it was only pictures and that 'don't' when I was trying to share my secret drawings with anyone. Now it was something real, action was needed.

And yes, I had doubts about my mental state. I ended up googling my symptoms and was not happy with the result. Apparently hearing voices and obsessive drawing is not the healthiest behavior when you are a teenager. So, once again, instead of having someone check my head, I just went along with the voice, forcing this strong "Don't." into our one-sided conversation.

On one side, I felt like a marionette, but on the other, it was making perfect sense. I was confident that I had a mission and that it was crucial for me to follow this lead. So, I did.

And here I was, standing on a bridge, filled with a crowd aligning to jump from it...? At least that's how it looked like. I tried to blend in, but she stopped me. Beautiful, tanned, covered with tattoos, flaming hot.

"Hey kid." She said, killing my mood. How could she call me that way? I was not a child and was going to be 17 very soon! "Are you here to jump?"

I looked around, figuring out my options. So, I was forced to come here, but had no idea what for. I looked around and apparently started to blush (awesome feature of my pale freckled skin in any stressful scenario) as the hot lady giggled, assuming I was just stunned by her look. Double embarrassment...

"I'm here to see someone..." I mumbled and was on my way to the girl, whose face was covered with the hood, glowing white-silver locks laying on her shoulders. She was extremely focused on her shoes, or the ground under her feet. It was hard to tell. She was waiting for her turn to jump. I looked around once more, trying to figure out if this extreme thing was something safe, or even legal. There were no doubts, it was her, exactly how I saw her, how I drew her for all those years. It was Sky.

I stepped closer and my invisible friend was not supporting this decision. It felt like I bumped into an invisible shield.

"Really?" I mumbled angrily. "You want me to stalk her?"

"Watch." Voice confirmed.

"We need to work on our communication, buddy!"

"Watch." Voice repeated impatiently.

"As you say." It was getting annoying. Was I crazy because I was listening to him?

I watched her moving slowly with the queue, standing close enough to see her and not to look like a stalker.

I held my breath when she was next, like I was the one to jump. I saw beautiful eyes finally looking up at the instructor in front of her... angrily. She didn't say anything, but I could definitely see the irritation on her face. He was saying something when it happened. A cloud of silver smoke rose from her and was moving toward the instructor. I looked at the reaction of people around, but no one else seemed to notice, or see it. Even Sky didn't seem to see it. Instructor was just staring at her, stunned, no attention to a cloud that was now blending in with his tanned skin.

I opened my mouth to say something. This was the next level of my weird quest. And then, within minutes of me staring at something only I saw, she jumped.

Apparently when you jump from the bridge, they don't pull you back up as I imagined. There was a small boat in a river, picking up the jumpers, disconnecting them from the rope and bringing them back to earth. I ran. It felt like right now it was time to finally talk to the girl, whose pictures were filling the album in my bag.

She just stood there, smiling, glowing, looking at the bridge she had just conquered. I didn't know how to start this weird conversation, but I couldn't stand aside any longer. I needed to talk to her.

"Sky?" I didn't need confirmation. I knew it was her. She looked at me puzzled for a couple of seconds. I felt goosebumps rushing through all my body. She smiled. Nothing needed to be told. She knew why I was here and who I was.

The moment I looked into her glowing eyes I realized the most important thing. I was not alone anymore.

• • • •

"I messed it up, didn't I?" We were sitting on the bench in a nearby park now, eating ice cream, purchased from a suspicious looking kiosk next to the bridge.

The voice was coming from her phone after she typed the words in. I didn't know that Sky didn't speak before we met, pictures in my head were failing to mention this. But I was not surprised. She gave it up, she made a choice. Like a little mermaid gave up her voice in exchange for her legs... but it was more complicated than this.

She pushed me with her elbow, seeing my mind being lost in comparison to my favorite cartoon and the very real girl sitting next to me.

"Yeah, you did." I concluded. "I saw it. Weird silver cloud attacking the guy on a bridge. That shouldn't happen."

I didn't know how it came to me, but when I was saying it, I felt a nod of approval from my invisible friend. Finally, we were on the same page here.

Sky looked at her ice cream with attention this crooked cone was not deserving.

"With great power comes great responsibility." I declared and almost choked, feeling disapproving grunt.

"Oh, shut up. It is a great quote." I whispered to my grumpy guide.

Sky looked at me like she knew something I didn't and typed in her phone: "What did you give up?"

"Nothing physical, I believe. Just a personal space." I chuckled feeling mental disapproval.

She looked at her almost finished ice cream now, probably judging if it was a fair trade for me. I was still not quite understanding if her trade was worth it, but I didn't want to ask yet. Just pulled my album from the backpack and gave it to her.

Sky opened it and started browsing through the pages, stopping on every one of them, connecting every picture with a memory she had. Here was a little Sky sitting on a bed with a book and shadow approaching her. Here was the small girl in school staring at the window. Here she was sitting in a park, hugging her knees under an ancient-looking tree. Nothing significant for me, but probably very crucial moments for her as her expressions were changing from smiley to sad within every page. And there was the last one. Sky standing on a bridge in front of a shadow of a guy she invaded just hours ago. The important one, the one that required me to see her after years of drawing.

"Can you fix it?" I pointed at the picture.

She nodded.

"Do you need help with it?" I was not sure how I could help her but felt a need to ask.

She smiled, probably thinking the same.

That was the day I finally met Sky.

• • • •

After meeting Sky, it all just fell into place. I was not a weirdo anymore, now I had an idea of what my gift was actually about.

Long conversations with her got me thinking. She was saying that we made a choice, that we gave up something important to be special, to have our abilities, to be a part of something bigger, to be important. I didn't recall making this kind of choice. Sky also said that when she was 'signing the contract' she was not aware of what would be taken from her, and only later realized that it would be her voice.

I was hoping it was not my case. First, I don't remember agreeing on anything. Second, it didn't look like I was missing anything. Also, my abilities were barely a gift. I just kept seeing pictures and was guided by the grumpy mumbling. It kept me wondering at that time.

And then I met Kim. It was different than with Sky. There were no picture seeing for her. I had no clue about her existence. It happened almost two years after the Sky's bridge incident. I was sitting in a café, stirring my coffee and staring at the people rushing on the street. Something clicked in my mind, and I heard a satisfied whisper in my head "This one."

I didn't need to clarify which one he was talking about and why he was so pleased with it. I learned not to ask many questions, they were very rarely answered anyway. But I didn't need to ask this time, I understood who he was talking about the moment I turned my head. She was passing next to me the moment I looked in the direction and I felt the shiver with all my body.

Even oversized jeans and a hoody couldn't hide the fact how slim and fit she was. A bit shorter than me, with shirt blond hair pulled in cute messy ponytail.

She sat behind the table not far from mine and pulled the notebook out of her backpack.

I stared for a couple of minutes, probably just being hypnotized by the grace of her movement and the beauty she was projecting. Even behind the wall of baggy clothes and huge earphones, I could see her, I could feel her.

She felt my stare and looked up. I didn't bother to look away and regretted it instantly. Black eyes seemed darker than charcoal and now were piercing through my soul.

She didn't smile, just barely visible tilted her head, intrigued.

"Go." My mental GPS advised, and I was happy to. Probably in any other case I would be shy to approach her. She was so far out of my league that I felt like I was trying to charm a celebrity. But I did what I've been told and in one moment I was standing next to her table, holding my paper cup.

She was not surprised or irritated, just kept watching me, with her head still tilted. I didn't say anything, seeing her not bothering with taking off her earphones. Just stood there like a shy kid. She waited and I just spread my hand in her direction. Handshake surprisingly felt as the safe way to start.

She looked at my hand like I was holding a grenade in it and I'm pretty sure I heard a chuckle in my head.

I was fighting the urge to take my hand back, to turn away and just leave the café, erasing this moment from my memory, but I couldn't. I just stood there next to a complete stranger with a desperate desire to be touched by her, which didn't make sense to me at that time. Not because it was so out of character to me, but because I never considered myself a tactile person before.

She halted for a couple of extremely long seconds, considering. Then slowly stretched her hand, putting it in mine. I felt her shiver once our skin touched, I noticed how she closed her eyes. It seemed like it brought her discomfort. Her hand felt cold, but sweaty at the same time. I was holding it and realized at the moment that I didn't want to let her go.

After one more awkward moment, she withdrew, and I noticed a faint smile on her face. She gestured to an empty seat next to her. She pulled her earphones off and I thought it was a good sign to start a real introduction, but when I opened my mouth, I heard this familiar grumpy breathing. I sat in the chair.

"My name is Kimberly... Kim." She said and her voice sounded like the high notes were taken from it, leaving it a bit blank and lifeless.

"Terrance...Ter." I said, smiling from the idea about how perfectly matching our names sounded. I imagined a fancy wedding invitation with "Kimberly & Terrance" engraved with golden cursive. Or the "Kim & Ter" scratched on the wood, inside the heart. Those were not the pictures I expected to see while introducing myself to a complete stranger. Pictures...

I held my breath, wondering if those were THE pictures? I chased those thoughts away. Since I met Sky, it was harder to differentiate 'the messages' with reality. She shifted from being a fantasy to being real, and now I had a tough time finding my thoughts in the flow of information I had.

Trying to clear up my head, I didn't notice the gap of silence awkwardly hanging in the air. Kim was just looking at my face with a smirk. Did she know what was happening in my head, was she able to get inside my mind like Sky could? I realized that I had no idea what gift she had... if any. From what I knew, she just could be a random normal girl, whom I should approach in the café because of the 'higher cause'. I smiled at this thought, realizing that probably I should find better terms for everything. I didn't know how to call a voice in my head or what my goal actually was. I just hoped that before I go crazy with all this, it will be clarified. Maybe I was crazy already...

Girl in front of me laughed softly, probably not understanding why the guy who dared to approach her was just sitting and not even starting a proper conversation, and instead just looking like his mind is shred into pieces.

"What is your curse?" She said with such a lightness, like she would while inquiring what do I want to drink.

I looked in the black eyes again, almost shivering from the power. These unbelievable eyes were staring straight in my soul. It felt dangerous, creepy even, but oddly satisfying.

"Curse." I echoed. I never thought of it this way as I never put together how it was affecting my life. Was it a terrible thing? I remembered Sky once again, forced to dive inside a man's mind to fix the damage she accidentally made. I remembered seeing her the next day after it was finally done. She was hurt, the ghost of a girl I saw blushing and shimmering with emotions under that bridge. Maybe it was her curse, maybe I also had one...

Kim kept looking at me with the same inquiring look.

"I see things..." The worst way to express what I was doing. "And hear a voice. I heard it just now before I saw you."

Kim smiled at me. She didn't think I was crazy, which already meant a world to me.

"And you can't stop it?" There was a glimmer of something in these eyes. Was it... hope?

"I haven't tried." I haven't tried to stop pictures or voices from invading my personal space. I haven't even thought of doing it until now. Maybe deep inside I believed that it was a part of me. I had it since I remembered and probably being without it... felt lonely. I mentally judged myself for not thinking about it before. Was I able to stop it? Should I go to doctor and receive a diagnosis for my condition?

"What was your cost?" Kim said, anticipating upcoming sadness.

Right, there should be a price I paid for 'being special'. But did I? Sky sacrificed her voice. What did I lose? Things were getting more confusing with her every word. She probably noticed it, saying, pointing at her right ear with a slim index finger:

"I can't hear. That was my price."

I looked at the big white earphones next to her on a table.

"I don't hear music, but I can sense vibrations."

"You don't sound like you're..." I didn't want to finish this sentence. Should I call her deaf? She didn't sound like it. In my imagination, it was pretty easy to identify a deaf person by the way they pronounce words, but Kim's speech was not like it. Her voice did sound a bit distant and less sharp, it felt like its roughness was smoothed. I didn't believe she was actually not hearing me. Next question arose:

"How do you understand me?"

She laughed: "Oh, you barely said anything aloud!"

It was true, since I sat at her table, I barely talked, absorbed in my internal struggle.

"I read lips. Most of the time it is enough. So please look in my direction if you want me to be a part of a conversation." She smiled again and sipped something from her cup.

"I don't know what was taken from me." I said, realizing that I didn't answer her previous question.

She raised the eyebrow.

"Did you meet anyone else?" I asked, wondering how many of us wandered around this planet. If it was at least 3 of us in one city, I would have hard time imagining actual worldwide numbers.

"No." She shook her head, probably wondering the same. Maybe she was not interested.

"There is Sky..." I started saying, focusing on keeping my lips in her direction, probably looking awkward and tense. "I met her couple of years ago and since that time we... meet..."

I didn't know how to describe our relationships better than that. It probably was sort of a business meeting, when she was asking questions about her life choices, and I was receiving answers from my internal guide. Or I was telling her what plans do 'they' have for her... She was blindly following it until now, even if it didn't make sense. She was so confident in those directions...

And here was Kim, filled with irony about 'the curse', considering if the price she paid was worth it. That would not be easy for me.

Kim issued a deep sight, saying: "That's where it's going now?" I knew what she was thinking. That I was here to trap her, to control her. I shook my head so suddenly that she flinched.

"I'm not here to force you into anything you don't want."

I immediately felt an unhappy roar in my head. Oh, yes, he didn't want me saying it, not according to universal plan, apparently.

Kim tilted her head, shifting her gaze from my lips to my eyes. That piercing stare. It felt like I was stabbed with the icicle straight through my soul.

"Aren't you?" She was genuinely surprised.

I felt grumpy mumbling again. For the first time in my life, I didn't care if I went against my goal. She was the one who planted this idea in my head, she was the one who had doubts about it and now I shared them with her. She was not Sky, I had no control over her, but since that moment she owned me.

• • • •

It took me about a month to find out what was Kim's gift. I knew that she was not a fan of touching people and could stare in their souls, but that was pretty much it.

"You're not going to tell me, aren't you?" I was giving it another shot. My curiosity was over the roof. We spent more time together than I could afford to. My mind was so busy with her constantly that I couldn't focus on anything else. I was quite sure that my boss would eventually fire me for my sloppy efforts to put together clumsy code and website designs. I barely spent enough time on it and was lucky to avoid punishment.

Every single minute I had, I wanted to spend with her. Whether chatting or cuddling. I needed her more than air as I was confident that oxygen is not needed when I'm next to her, hugging her, smelling her hair, touching her skin. Being separated from her felt not only lonely, but it also felt painful. I don't know if she felt the same, but she never said no to me. Not when I texted her in the middle of night while I was struggling to sleep, not when I was introducing myself to her father, not when I kissed her for the first time...

She looked at me, tilting her head. Same way she did the day we met, considering.

"Why do you need to know?" She probably thought that I lied to her before, that I wanted to use her, that I didn't plan to go against the voice.

"I want to understand you better."

Surprisingly, the voice was not around when I was next to Kim. Probably hiding, patiently waiting for the right moment. Was I mindlessly following its plan by falling desperately in love with this girl? Probably...

"It's me, it's not it..." I said apologetically. It felt like the truth, at least.

I saw her studying her freshly painted pink fingernails for the moment.

We were sitting on the beach, with our shoes off, bare feet in the water, enjoying the sunset.

"I can see future." She dropped like it was not a big deal.

"It makes both of us." I chuckled.

"You can see only Sky and me. I see everyone I touch. Not far, only the nearest... months or two..."

"That's kind of cool." I dropped without actually thinking it through.

It took me a moment to realize that she knew what we were going to become the moment she touched me in the café the day we met. She hesitated than, didn't want to touch me... like she still does with every single human, apart from me and her father. I never saw her touching anyone. There was a reason behind it and still looking at her nails, Kim whispered, not looking at me, not willing to listen to what I had to say.

"I've seen death..."

It hit me. Kim never appeared to me as broken and fragile, until this moment. I silently pulled her into a hug and felt her breathing deeper, probably forcing herself not to cry. I wanted her to cry, I wanted her to spill it on me, her secrets, her emotions. I knew she never talked about it with anyone else, I felt it. I kissed the top of her head, and she tucked her face into my chest, listening to my heart racing.

I didn't expect her to, but she continued talking: "I can make choices... when future splits into options, I can make a choice for someone..."

I shook my head, not quite getting it. She probably felt it.

"When you have a decision to make. Like to eat soup or omelet... I can choose. I'm able to force you either way and you would believe that it was your decision, even if originally it wasn't. I can take away the freedom of choice..."

Her voice became barely audible in that last part. Chills ran all over my body. I was thinking of hundreds and thousands of times that we were making choices... Kim was able to override them. Now I knew why she was delaying this conversation.

If people knew about her gift, what would they think? Would they be afraid of a girl who can make them do basically anything, who can take their freedom from them? Probably, yes.

• • • •

"Do you think they did it in purpose?" I was sitting in bed, scribbling something I didn't yet understand in my notebook.

Kim was not looking at me, so the question died in the air. I was still doing it all the time, forgetting how special she is, not checking if she's reading my lips the moment I randomly start talking.

I looked at her face half hidden under the blanket. Her black eyes picked up that movement immediately, and she turned my way, smiling.

I could continue burying this question inside of me, but I shouldn't.

"Do you think they planned 'us'?" I rephrased, following with the wide gesture, confirming that I was talking about our relationships.

She smiled again. It was more like an ironic smirk this time. It was not a question and we both knew it. Of course it was their plan.

"It was not a choice for any of us…" She whispered and it finally hit me.

Kim knew it from the beginning. The moment I touched her in that café, she knew that whatever was happening between us was meant to be.

"Isn't it boring to know everything in advance?" I teased.

She shook her head. No, it was not, and I felt silly even asking it now.

"It's nowhere near boring. Even worse. It's addictive to know. I wish I could know more than the nearest future, just to know that something good will last and bad will finish soon. But I take as much as they give me."

"If you take." I teased her, reminding her that most of the time she avoided contact with other people.

"If they give." Her lips were still partly hidden under the blanket, but I saw her smiling.

I still didn't know how it was working with her gift and was not going to ask, unless she was ready to slip information. Now I knew that she didn't see everything. Interesting.

• • • •

Kim was sitting on the couch on her house porchway when I was approaching. Cup of something warm in her hands, feet tucked in under blanket, eyes distant, staring somewhere.

She didn't turn to me until I touched her shoulder.

"What's happening?" I swallowed a tension building up in my throat.

For a couple of seconds, she still looked into my eyes with that terrifying blank expression. She was sitting in front of me, but I knew that her mind was elsewhere.

She blinked slowly and a lively glow finally appeared on her face.

"You should not be the one asking this question." She smiled with her eyes. So many feelings were there now that I could barely catch the stream. Happy to see me, but sad because something was going to happen, tangled with the heavy doom of carrying her gift.

I hated myself for doing it, for putting her through this experience again. She hated making other people's choices and I was the messenger. I was the one who was forcing her to do it... again... I was wondering if she was still going to like me after years of me doing this to her. I was wondering if she loved me the same way I loved her... We still never raised this tricky relationships and feelings subject. I was wondering if she knew what I was thinking about it for days.

She smiled, more genuinely this time, obviously making an effort to look happier than she was.

I took a seat in the chair next to her, buying myself time, trying to figure it out without chasing this smile from her face.

It's your mission again. I flipped through images in my mind which were still surprisingly clear.

"Sky needs to make a choice."

I think I saw a barely visible nod, or I was just imagining it. Kim turned away from me once again, staring at something only she could see.

"I thought they have future..." She mumbled. "They're a weird couple. But he loves her so badly and he takes her in the way she is, even if she's hurting him. She makes him happy even despite causing him damage... So weird, but it was meant to be."

"Until now, I guess." I was not able to hide the ironic smile. I also thought that Sky and Max would be together longer. "She needs to stop it."

Kim nodded again, barely visible: "It will be so painful... at least for him..."

We both knew Sky was not in love with Max and breaking up would not cause her so much pain as it would to him.

"If I tell her to do it..." I stumbled, breathing in deeper.

"She will tell you to go to hell and deal with your relationships instead. And she will continue being with Max to prove a point, I guess."

She shook her head, probably weighing her choices again and continued with her voice cracking: "I will do it..."

"I will never tell her you did." I know it wouldn't help, that Kim will still feel like shit for days after adjusting Sky's choice, after changing future, after causing this pain to Max. I knew it and I hated myself for being a reason for her doing it.

"I don't want to do it anymore." Kim whispered, showing for a split second all the range of emotions she felt right now, but tucking them in under the surface as soon as she could, issuing a barely genuine smile.

"I know, Babe, and I'm so sorry." I dropped on my knees next to her, taking her cold hands with mine and kissing them, trying to warm it with my lips.

I will be there for her until she feels like herself again and then we will be fine, we will be happy again... Right until the moment it happens again.

• • • •

"Nooo." I woke up with this word on my lips, in my mind. "NOOO." It repeated again, probably to make sure that I didn't miss it.

"What is it?" I asked automatically. It was dark outside, probably around 1 am, I assumed.

I looked at Kim curling under the blanket on the other side of the bed. Even while she was asleep, she was trying her best not to touch me. What was she afraid to see in my future?

"Spill it." I mumbled, dropping my feet on the floor. The voice was exceedingly rare in my head in Kim's presence, so it should be something urgent.

"Kim." It confirmed.

"What about her?" I was annoyed.

"Her service is needed." It was probably the longest sentence voice ever put together.

"What?"

135

"Choice needs to be made." One more surprisingly long sentence.

"She doesn't want to use her power." I pronounced it like always, even though I knew voice would hear me even if I only thought of it.

"Choice should be made." More insistent this time.

"I will not ask her to do it." I resisted. Not within days of seeing her broken... again. "She will not do it..." Even without asking I knew it. I could easily imagine her piercing black eyes staring at me like I was not the one she knew and trusted. This would be a betrayal. I would never betray her...

"Choice should be made." Voice repeated more patiently this time. Again, and again...

• • • •

"Ter..." I heard Kim behind my back. The sunrise view was beautiful. I sat on the balcony, holding a lit cigarette between my fingers.

"What's wrong?" It took her a few brief seconds of looking at my exhausted face to understand that I was not well.

Since I woke up hours ago, voice haven't stopped repeating the same phrase over and over again. I couldn't do anything about it, there was no way to block it as it was invading my mind, drowning any other thought that was trying to appear instead. I was not able to fight it.

I felt angry. At the voice taking over control of my mind, at myself for becoming so close to Kim and willing to suffer this for her, to protect her. I felt drained, like it hasn't been only a couple of hours, but days or even weeks since I was under pressure.

I didn't know what to say, how to explain it to her. I didn't know if I needed to as the emptiness of her black eyes was already staring straight to my soul.

"You are making a choice." She whispered.

"It is not a choice." I shook my head, trying to shake away the pressure.

"You are choosing... for me."

I didn't dare look into those eyes. Something I could never hide from her was making a choice. She sensed it.

Pain in my head reached the stage when I was not able to resist it anymore, I felt tears streaming down my cheeks.

"Don't." I whispered. "Don't look at it." I didn't want her to know what I was trying to do, how I was trying to protect her. My voice felt foreign to myself. It seamed like I was talking from the depth of the well: "It wants you to change someone's choice."

Kim took a step behind in a genuine desire to protect herself, leave, hide from me. Did she believe that I would break my promise and force her into something she didn't want?

"I'm not letting you do it." I heard my voice cracking, it felt like my scull was doing the same.

Kim looked at me like I was not the man she knew, like she hasn't just stepped out from my bed.

"You're fighting for me..." I saw a spark of admiration on her face and then I closed my eyes and was swallowed by the darkness.

• • • •

It was hard to open my eyes, but I managed. Kim was sitting next to me in bed, and I was immediately curious how she managed to pull me here from the balcony.

"It's gone." I whispered.

She nodded.

"Choice was made. There is no way back now."

"You didn't..."

"I didn't affect it, but I know what it was all about. It was about Sky, that's why your voice was so insistent. She... went sideways from 'the plan.'"

"They wanted her to choose differently..."

"Not her... Ben."

"Who is Ben?"

"I'm not sure. I know that he is the one who chose, and it will crucially affect her life apparently."

"Is it bad?" I almost felt bad that we refused to help. Maybe it would lead to catastrophe.

"Choices are tricky..." Kim mumbled staring at the picture on the wall, like she was talking to it, not me.

"Kim..." I whispered, but quickly realized that she didn't hear me, still watching the mountains meeting sunset. I touched her shoulder and felt her flinching under my palm.

Her deep eyes were full of tears within a second. Did it hurt? My touch? I removed my hand, just in case.

"What's wrong?" I asked looking at the stream appearing on her cheek.

"You made a choice... Now you have the price."

"What is it?" I was shocked, but ready to accept the consequences.

"Us." It was barely audible, but in my imagination this one word echoed all over the room.

"No…" I shook my head. "They waited for the moment until I have something… someone meaningful in my life to announce my price for this f*cking curse? Nooo!" I punched my mattress and my hand bounced back.

• • • •

I still consider it the best thing I have ever done. I gave her freedom, I fought for her like the prince in a stupid fairytale. Did I win? That is the other question.

I wish it would go other way, and the price would not be that big.

She is free now, hopefully for a long time. I'm pretty sure that soon they will try again, probably as soon as they have something or someone to pressure her with. Someone important enough, so she will give up.

Kim didn't have 'duty' now, but I still had. It was only Sky now, and her life was taking a leap of faith. Ben was there now in the way he shouldn't be, apparently.

"He is my uncle." We were sitting in the darkest and farthest corner of our diner, when she declared it, something similar to doubt on her face.

I nodded, sipping my coffee, trying to hide my actual reactions.

"I am having secret relationships with him." Sky stared at me, not realizing why I was not shocked the way she expected.

"Yes, you are." I nodded.

"What aren't you telling me, Ter?"

Well, I was never good at hiding.

139

"Don't." Voice whispered and I blindly obeyed.

I stared at my half empty cup.

"Sorry, I'm just not feeling my best lately."

Selective truth, but still a truth. I did feel like my life was missing sense now. It's been couple of days since I played my prince role and paid my price. It was taking effect slowly. Now when I was looking at Kim, I saw a stunning young woman, but she was out of range. I still wanted to touch and kiss her, but when I did... it just felt like I'm taking something that is not mine. I guess she felt similar as we got oddly distant lately. But that was a price, and I was paying it willingly.

It would take Sky a moment to dive into my head and know the truth, but she didn't. I believe she never did. Was there a mental wall created by the voice, which she was not able to pass, or was it just respect to my personal space?

But she knew exactly the only thing that could cause me to be this way.

"Kim?"

"She's alright." I said confidently. "Us... it's complicated." I felt my voice cracking in the middle of the sentence. We were never complicated before. Our relationships were the easiest I've ever had.

Sky nodded, not wanting to dig deeper. Good that she had her staff to worry about now. If she had her full focus, she would never let it go this way.

I cleared my throat: "Whatever Max offers, you need to go ahead with it."

That's why we met today. I got a message for Sky. Not an extremely detailed one, though.

Sky raised her brows. I did the same with my shoulders.

"I don't know... That's all I've got."

"What is this game?" She typed, looking around, like it was the first time she noticed her surroundings. Maybe she did, considering how absorbed she was with her new weird relationships.

"It's not a game..." I just couldn't look at her now. Or was it? I often had a feeling like I was a tool in someone else's hands.

• • • •

"I'm going with you." The message just showed up on my phone screen. Just like that. After almost a month of silence. A month, every day of each I had these weird mixed feelings.

"I can see your choices." Another message followed.

I waited. I really wanted to see her, but the idea of the emotions it might cause. I didn't even know what I felt to Kim anymore.

It was weird to meet Sky and technically tell her nothing. They wanted her to think that she was off the hook, that her 'Ben situation' was in her hands. Funny. After what we've been through with Kim, after forcing Sky to jump through the hoops, they were trying to pretend that it was not that important after all. That it was never about Sky and Ben. Ridiculous.

I never responded to that text.

• • • •

Everything slowed down when I saw Kim. Smiling, joking, teasing me calling by my full name. It all felt so real. I followed her lead. I played her game. I played my part as I usually did. I missed her so much.

But it was not about us, not yet. We were there to lie to Sky, which was not the easiest thing to do.

It felt draining just to be there, just to fake enthusiasm, to promise her something she couldn't have, to tell her that she was free.

But none of us were free. Kim, maybe, for now at least, until the moment they find the new leverage, until they get to her. I hope I will always be able to protect her.

Also by Alinar Den

Two Souls in One Body
Reaching Sky
No Flowers?